The Rivals of Casper Road

ROAN PARRISH

*Will a nightmare competition
make his dreams come true?*

HARLEQUIN
SPECIAL EDITION

**Believe in love. Overcome obstacles.
Find happiness.**

*Relate to finding comfort and strength in the
support of loved ones and enjoy the journey
no matter what life throws your way.*

AVAILABLE THIS MONTH

ISBN-13: 978-1-335-72420-5

**THE MAVERICK'S
MARRIAGE PACT**
STELLA BAGWELL

**THE COWGIRL AND
THE COUNTRY M.D.**
CATHERINE MANN

**THE RIVALS OF
CASPER ROAD**
ROAN PARRISH

**THE MARINE'S
CHRISTMAS WISH**
JOANNA SIMS

LONDON CALLING
DARBY BAHAM

**HER GOOD-LUCK
CHARM**
ELIZABETH BEVARLY

HSEATMIFC0922

Suddenly, Zachary had the creeping sense that they'd wandered into a horror movie.

It would be revealed that there was no Mrs. Lundy. That the piles of stones and sticks birthed themselves on the locations of each person whom Mrs. Lundy's ghost drained of life force to stay haunting this hideous sixties minimalism.

He giggled at the idea.

"What?" Bram asked, as if he'd welcome the chance to be included in a joke.

"Nothing. Just imagining that this would make a really good start to a horror movie."

"Well, at least I would live," Bram said seriously. "Because I'm a virgin."

Zachary blinked, torn between surprise at Bram's comment and surprise that he knew that trope when he didn't watch horror movies.

The latter was more interesting.

"I thought you didn't watch horror movies?" Zachary asked.

"I might've googled after your impassioned speech."

Zachary was touched.

"It's interesting. Maybe we could watch one some time and you can tell me about all the tropes. But *not* a super scary one," he said intently.

This had taken an unexpected turn and he didn't know what to think about it.

"We could do that," Zachary murmured.

Dear Reader,

Autumn is my favorite time of the year—the fiery leaves, the scent of wood smoke and apples in the air, and most of all, Halloween. Like the season, Halloween is a holiday about transformation and embracing the abandon of our dark and wild shadow selves.

The Rivals of Casper Road pits new Garnet Run arrival Bram Larkspur against reigning champion Zachary Glass in a neighborhood Halloween decorating contest. Bram is as open and sunny as Zachary is private and intense, and what begins as a competition escalates to a prank war...and then transforms into love.

For me, the magic of Halloween is that it allows us to try on different versions of ourselves—provocative, playful, experimental versions that have the power to reveal to us who we really are and what we want. For Bram and Zachary, Halloween does just that. They want a life they can dream into being together.

The gang is all here, so you'll get to check in with the couples from the rest of the series as you watch Bram and Zachary fall in love. Welcome back to Garnet Run, Wyoming. I hope you'll stay awhile!

Cozy reading,

<3 *Roan*

RoanParrish.com

The Rivals of
Casper Road

——

ROAN PARRISH

HARLEQUIN
SPECIAL
EDITION

HARLEQUIN®
SPECIAL
EDITION™

PLEASE RECYCLE
THIS PRODUCT IS RECYCLABLE

Recycling programs
for this product may
not exist in your area.

ISBN-13: 978-1-335-72420-5

The Rivals of Casper Road

Copyright © 2022 by Roan Parrish

For questions and comments about the quality of this book, please contact us at CustomerService@Harlequin.com.

Harlequin Enterprises ULC
22 Adelaide St. West, 41st Floor
Toronto, Ontario M5H 4E3, Canada
www.Harlequin.com

Printed in U.S.A.

Roan Parrish lives in Philadelphia, where she's gradually attempting to write love stories in every genre. When not writing, she can be found cutting her friends' hair, meandering through the city while listening to torch songs and melodic death metal, or cooking overly elaborate meals. She loves bonfires, winter beaches, minor chord harmonies, and self-tattooing. One time she may or may not have baked a six-layer chocolate cake and then thrown it out the window in a fit of pique.

Books by Roan Parrish

Harlequin Special Edition

The Garnet Run series
The Lights of Knockbridge Lane

Carina Press

The Garnet Run series
Best Laid Plans
Better Than People

Visit the Author Profile page
at Harlequin.com for more titles.

Garnet Run

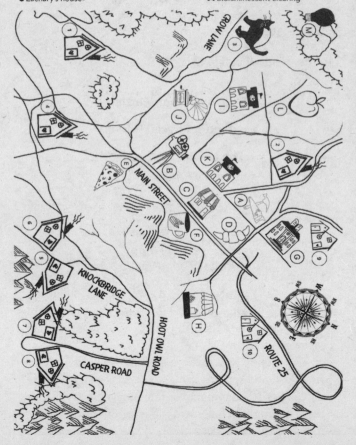

Chapter One

Bram

He'd chosen it because of the name: Casper Road. Recently Bram Larkspur had felt like a ghost. At least a friendly one would be an upgrade.

After six months of working at Hollywell's Tree Farm half an hour north and housesitting for its owner, he'd gotten a tip that Garnet Run was a nice place to be. Cheap, picturesque, and possessed of a more robust queer community than you might expect for a small town in Wyoming.

The money he'd saved was more than enough for first, last, and security, so he'd rented the small house on Casper Road and moved his meager possessions there the night before, arriving after dark and falling into an exhausted sleep.

The August morning dawned, lazy and warm, and Bram felt his heart settle just a little; felt it beat, snugged safe within the protective cage of his ribs.

For a while there, he'd worried it might be irreparably broken.

But that was six months ago. Now, he told himself, he had a new life in a new town on a new street, and he didn't want to waste a minute of it.

He whistled and Hemlock, his yellow Labrador, pranced into the room, brown eyes warm and familiar. Bram scratched between her ears and Hem put her front paws on his knees, whuffling enthusiastically. He kissed her head and she licked his elbow, as usual.

"Let's go explore," Bram said.

Hem yipped with excitement.

Casper Road was a curvy three-quarters of a mile, ending in the cul-de-sac near Bram's house. At the other end, it dead-ended into Hoot Owl Road. The houses on Casper Road were of all different sizes and styles, and the road seemed to have grown in order to connect the houses rather than the other way around.

The most notable thing about it, though, was the way most houses contained "Casper Road" in their address plaques. No "745" here; it was all "745 Casper Road." A few even had ghosts next to the numbers.

Bram and Hemlock spent a pleasant half hour walking up and back the street slowly, noting the gardens and trees (Bram) and sticks and smells (Hemlock). When they got back to number 667, Bram fed Hemlock, made some dandelion tea, and took his tea and his whittling bag back outside to watch Casper Road awake.

Bram settled on the front stoop. Hemlock snuffed

around the steps for a while, then settled beside him, half of her on each step.

Bram had been whittling since he was ten, the only one of his five siblings to catch the bug. He'd been transfixed watching his father transform chunks of wood into art. For years, he'd begged to try it, and had always been told, "Watch. Learn." Then, on his tenth birthday, he'd unwrapped a chunk of basswood and a pair of thick gloves.

"Where's the knife?" Bram had said, fingers itching to hold wood and blade.

"You get the knife when you promise us that you'll always wear the gloves while you whittle," his father had said.

"I promise," Bram had sworn solemnly, and his mother had produced a knife from behind her back. She'd laughed with joy at his excitement and his father had said, "Carve me something pretty."

They weren't the same gloves, of course, but Bram had always kept his promise. Even a thousand miles from his parents, he pulled on his gloves before he picked up the knife.

"What are you going to be?" he murmured to the chunk of wood he'd plucked from the curb on their morning walk. He let his mind and eyes wander as he thought.

Bram didn't know anything about architecture, but the black-and-white house across from his looked odd. It seemed to have flown together rather at random until you unfocused your eyes and then it was clear that its symmetry was diagonal rather than horizontal. Bram found it both ugly and intriguing, but the more he looked at it the more ugly gave way to intrigue.

Sometimes when Bram whittled, the whole world went away. Other times, it was just something to do with his hands. This morning, it was the latter, and he carved into the wood as he contemplated the diagonal house and the stirrings up and down Casper Road.

What emerged was a pelican, the swoop of its beak breaking the diagonal of the wood. Bram smoothed his blade along its back and Hemlock farted in her sleep.

"Back to normal, then," Bram muttered, turning his face away from her.

"Welcome, neighbor!"

A man was approaching from the left. He was white, appeared to be in his sixties, and was wearing shorts and a cowboy hat, a combination that Bram found cartoonish. But he was smiling as he held out his hand to shake, and Bram could never spurn a smile.

"Hey, I'm Bram Larkspur. Nice to meet you."

He shook the man's hand with his whittling glove on before he realized it. The gloves felt so much a part of him. But the man didn't seem to mind any. He looked at the wood in Bram's other hand.

"That an eagle? No. What're them things called?"

"A pelican. At least, that's what it seems like," Bram said. You didn't tell the wood what it wanted to be. The wood told you with every whorl and grain.

"That's right, that's right. I'm Carl Former, live right there." He pointed to the house next door on the left. "Been here about fifteen years, so if you need anything you just let me know."

"Thank you, that's really kind."

"You're not from around here, I don't think?" Carl asked it as a question, but he was peering at Bram as if trying to parse his not-from-around-here-ness before Bram even answered.

"No. I'm from Washington State. Olympia. I moved to Sundance Junction in the winter to help on a tree farm, but after the season ended I made my way down here."

That was all true. But like most true things, it could have been said completely differently and been truer. He could have said, *I lived in Olympia until my boyfriend and my best friend tore my life and my heart in half, leaving me a broken person who had to get away in order to keep things together.*

But although Bram's siblings liked to tease him about being too open with people, even Bram knew that this neighbor wasn't the person to share that with.

Besides, he had put it behind him. He was in Garnet Run now and he wasn't the same person who'd had his heart ripped out, chewed to pieces, and shoved back in his chest to beat sideways as a constant reminder that the people you trusted and loved the most were the ones with the power to destroy you.

Yeah, it was totally behind him.

"Hey, there!" called a woman from across the street. She'd come out to her mailbox and was now crossing to Bram and Carl. "I'm Charlotte Banks, nice to meetcha." She held out her hand and Bram gave another gloved shake, then took off his gloves and put down his knife. If he was going to be meeting the neighbors, perhaps brandishing a knife wasn't the best way to do it.

"Was Carl telling you about Halloween?"

"Er, no?"

"Every Halloween, Casper Road holds a contest for who has the best Halloween decorations. The local kids all know about it, so everyone comes here to trick-or-treat. The local news covers it. It's a lot of fun! And since you're one of us now…"

Bram smiled. That was a fun idea, and perhaps explained the ghostly Casper Road enthusiasm that he'd seen on people's mailboxes and address plaques.

"When do you start?"

"Whenever you want," Carl said. "Mags and I don't put quite as much into it as we once did. But we'll still plan our decorations a few weeks before. The Shertslingers at the end of the cul-de-sac go all out. They've got three kids who get pretty into it. Michael and Jean really do it up big too."

"But Zachary Glass…well…"

"Yes, Zachary…"

Carl and Charlotte shared a look and then made the universal face of one performatively choosing not to speak ill of another.

"Zachary Glass?" Bram asked. It sounded like a supervillain name in one of the comics his sister Birch was always reading.

They both pointed at the diagonal house across the street that Bram had contemplated earlier.

As if the weight of their combined stares could conjure solid matter, the door to number 666 Casper Road opened and a man emerged.

He was slender and of medium height, with an olive complexion and thick, curly black hair. He wore a light gray suit, black wingtips, and a light pink shirt and tie even though it was 8:30 on a Saturday morning.

Carl and Charlotte waved at him and the man descended the steps and crossed the street toward them.

He had an awkward way of moving, as if he weren't quite comfortable in his own skin.

"Hello. You just moved in."

It wasn't a question, and the man didn't hold out a hand to shake. In fact he seemed to be inspecting Bram rather than welcoming him.

"Bram Larkspur."

Bram stuck out a hand, curious what the man would do.

"I'm Zachary Glass."

Zachary shook his hand, and his grip was firm but not aggressive and he let go quickly, like he was sealing a business deal.

Up close, he was interesting-looking. His face was all hard angles and dramatic dark eyebrows, but his mouth was lush and soft, and his eyelashes were a dark and elegant sweep. His brown eyes looked sharp and intelligent.

"We were just telling Bram here about the Casper Road Halloween Decorating Contest. Really you should talk to Zachary. He's won it every year since he moved onto Casper Lane," Carl said.

A proud smile played at the corners of Zachary's mouth.

"Yes," he confirmed.

"Seems like you start to plan the next year bright and early November 1st," Charlotte said, clearly trying to include Zachary in the light and jokey tone of the conversation.

But Zachary just said, "I take a day off after winning. To enjoy it."

Bram wondered if this buttoned-up guy ever enjoyed anything. But then Zachary broke into a real smile, revealing very white teeth that overlapped charmingly, and his face was transformed.

"Wait until you see what I've got planned for this year."

Bram revised his opinion. There was an impish delight about him.

"What've you got planned?" Bram asked.

"You'll see," Zachary said, raising an inky eyebrow.

Bram snorted.

"You'll join in the fun, won't you?" Charlotte asked.

Bram had never cared much for Halloween, but he loved making things, and loved festivals and parades, so surely it would be fun to participate in something that would bring costumed trick-or-treaters. Besides, if he was going to be living here now, it would be an excellent way to make friends.

So he nodded. "Yeah. Yeah, I absolutely will."

Carl grinned. Charlotte beamed.

Zachary Glass narrowed his eyes, all traces of his smile gone. Now, it seemed, he was evaluating the competition.

Chapter Two

Zachary

A variable had entered Zachary Glass' meticulously planned life. And it had a dog.

Zachary closed the front door behind him and returned to his plans. The building he was working on had some challenges, structurally, that he needed to work out. It was designed to be built against a rock face and the effect was to be almost as though it had been carved out of the mountain itself. The tension between the crushing solidity of rock and the delicate lines of the excised structure gave the piece an immediacy that sent shivers up Zachary's spine.

He loved this. The art of the edifice. It was art on the largest scale. And to see one of his buildings in the world? He couldn't think of anything more rewarding.

Except perhaps his annual Halloween decorating victory.

The other inhabitants of Casper Road were really no competition. Most of them participated for fun; some threw up some store-bought decorations a few days before Halloween and a few enjoyed the project enthusiastically. But even the most elaborate decorations among them were for maximalist effect, and none could hold a candle to the meticulously planned concepts that took up all of Zachary's spare time when he let it. Which he always did. But although the judges saw his visions, some of his neighbors remained huffy about their loss.

A few years ago, the second time Zachary won, Tracy Breslin at the end of the cul-de-sac questioned his victory.

"It's just so...weird," had been her articulate complaint. "And it's *not* festive."

"The festival of All Hallows' Eve was dedicated to honoring the dead and came from Samhain, during which the cattle would be brought down from the summer pastures and slaughtered for sustenance through the winter," Zachary had informed her and the neighbors that had gathered, magnetized by controversy. "And open burial mounds are no weirder than mass-produced plastic models of human skeletons, surely."

Tracy Breslin had sniffed, raised her eyebrows as if to say that she was very much not convinced of this argument, and headed for home. That had been the last time someone had challenged Zachary's win to his face, but likely not the last time they'd done so behind his back.

His neighbors were probably fine, as neighbors went.

Zachary didn't know and he didn't care. But as designers they left much to be desired. In fact the only one of them that Zachary considered competition was old Mrs. Lundy near the intersection of Casper Road and Hoot Owl Road. Her strange piles of sticks and stones were truly chilling. When the sun was at certain places in the sky, they cast shadows that Zachary was convinced were conjurations in their own right.

But no one else—not neighbors, the trick-or-treaters, or the judges from the local paper—seemed to take any notice of them. Instead, they always awarded second and third place to designs that looked like a seasonal Halloween store had disgorged itself. A nauseating mishmash of premade graves and spiderwebs and fabric, lit by garish lights and billowing in the wind to the cacophonous soundtrack of howling, evil laughter, and doors desperately in need of WD-40.

But, as they only got second and third place, Zachary didn't care.

Standing at his drafting table, he could see the new arrival to Casper Road sunnily glad-handing with every neighbor who passed by. Of course, they weren't simply passing by. Carl had no doubt texted Beverly Mathers, his partner in neighborhood crime—and by crime, Zachary meant utterly placid, crime-free gossip—who had activated the Casper Road Phone Tree, a complex and arcane system that somehow managed to keep certain people always in the know and others (including—and perhaps limited to—Zachary himself) in the dark.

Which, on measure, was precisely where he would choose to be, if given the choice.

But his exclusion from the phone tree, like most of

the other exclusions in his life, had not been his choice, even if it was one of the less painful ones.

Zachary rose at 6:30 as always. He did his stretching, his exercises, and stretched again. He took a shower and dressed. He considered himself in the mirror: slim, average height, ordinary. Nothing to invite the torment he had once received. No more laughable clothes. No more hand-me-down shoes with flapping soles. No more "Aren't Jews supposed to be rich?" comments.

But his face, well. He couldn't look at it without hearing those voices more than a decade in the past. He couldn't see his curly brown hair without hearing them say "Pubes." Couldn't look at his olive complexion without hearing "Where are you from and why don't you go back there?" Couldn't see his nose—which he was pretty sure was of an average size—without hearing the nickname that had begun in elementary school for reasons that were obvious but never made explicit: Captain Hook. The Jewish pirate.

His brown eyes were sharp, focused. The eyes of someone who got things done. Someone who looked at the past and said, "Bah." No. Someone who didn't even look.

Zachary had been told that he was nice-looking. He'd even been pretty sure the people who'd said it had meant what they'd said. But it didn't matter. The words had entered him like fishhooks when his skin was thin, and his tender mind held on to everything. They were lodged beneath the surface now—they sat like tattoo ink, six layers deep.

And mostly he was fine with it. It wasn't like looks

were an important part of architecture. Mostly he didn't think about it. But every morning, when he got dressed and combed his hair, he took one moment to look in the mirror and make sure that the kid who had drawn all those horrible comments was nowhere to be seen.

He tied his brown brogues and walked to the mailbox. He did this every morning. The United States Postal Service was the last bastion of infrastructure in a world crumbling from the inside out and he took comfort in its regularity.

He had multiple pen pals, subscribed to three architecture journals, four horror magazines, and *Martha Stewart Living* (shut up), and he enjoyed the anticipation of the walk to the curb, the slow opening of the mailbox, like unwrapping a present but without the waste of wrapping paper.

He pulled out the mail and was delighted to see a manila envelope from his favorite eBay store. He opened the envelope carefully and slid the vintage 1983 October issue of *Fangoria* out. He'd bought it for an interview with Vincent Price and John Carpenter's article about the music of *Halloween*. It whispered *Read me* to him, but Zachary couldn't indulge it until after work. It would be his reward.

There was also a fat envelope from Penelope, one of his pen pals.

It was a good mail day. Often, that meant it was going to be a good day all around.

"You work early, huh? Do you commute?"

The voice was unfamiliar and therefore immediately identifiable as the new neighbor's. He was clearly not from Wyoming, given that he didn't sound like he was from Wyoming and also that he thought 7:30 a.m. was early to go to work.

Zachary turned slowly.

The man—Bram; he knew his name was Bram— had the kind of messy blond-brown hair that Zachary associated with surfers or people who went to music festivals, but although Bram might not have been from Wyoming he looked like a lumberjack through and through, from the broad shoulders, muscular arms and chest, and the beard through which his white teeth gleamed in a smile.

"I work from home," Zachary said.

"Ha-ha." Bram's smile lit up his bright blue eyes and made the faintest wrinkles around them.

Zachary frowned. What part of that could possibly have been interpreted as funny?

"I do."

Bram faltered.

"Oh, sorry. I thought you were joking cuz of..." His gesture encompassed Zachary's whole body. "You really dress like that to work from home?"

"I'm a professional. I dress like a professional. Productivity has been proven to be affected by dress in those who work from home. Besides," he added. "I have video meetings."

Bram ran a hand through his hair. "You look nice. I didn't mean anything by it. I just never imagined someone would dress like that unless they had to." He winced at himself. "It just seems uncomfortable."

"It's not," Zachary said simply, ignoring the rub of his right shoe against the thin skin at the back of his heel. They were just new and not quite worn in yet, that was all.

"Sure. Cool."

But Bram kept standing there as if he expected something from Zachary.

"Are you enjoying Garnet Run?" Zachary asked, a concession to politeness that he felt would be enough to make a good impression before he never spoke to this man again.

But instead of the pat answer that Zachary had come to expect from most people, a shadow crossed Bram's handsome face. It was much more appealing, the shadow.

"Yeah, I... I was living in Sundance Junction for a few months before I came here. Me and Hemlock."

He scratched the dog's ears as he spoke, and the lab's eyes closed in ecstasy as her mouth lolled open.

"It was... Well, I just had to get out of Olympia. But I miss it. My family. I've never lived away from them before. It's been hard."

Zachary wished that his knee-jerk thought was what it usually would be: *Okay, Captain Overshare, I didn't actually need your life story. See ya never.*

But the sadness in Bram's eyes, the loss that he clearly felt at being separated from his family, was undeniable.

Personally, Zachary couldn't relate. But it was clear Bram's family was nothing like his own.

"Why'd you leave, then?"

Bram looked over Zachary's shoulder toward the mountains that rose behind.

"Just...couldn't be there anymore."

He opened his mouth like he was about to say more, and Zachary felt it happen: the cringing squirm of self-consciousness that he used to feel often—when the other kids teased him, when they stared at him; when confronted with someone he thought was attractive.

But it hadn't happened in a long time. Because he wasn't a schoolkid anymore. And because long ago he'd begun to avoid the people that made his knees go weak with attraction. Besides, it turned out that a lot of super-hot people? Were also mega-assholes. Correlation might not have been causation, but correlation was enough to want to stay the hell away from them.

But here was Bram, handsome as the day was long, and seemingly not incapable of human kindness.

Damn it.

"I gotta go," Zachary muttered, more to himself than to Bram.

He straightened his shoulders, drew himself up to his full (admittedly not very great) height, and said with as much ceremony as he could muster, "Good day, Abraham."

"Bram," Bram corrected, and Zachary had no idea why he'd decided to call the man by his full name when he'd introduced himself as something else. Only a total asshole doesn't call someone what they want to be called, speaking of assholes.

"Excuse me," Zachary apologized.

"No, I just mean, it's not short for Abraham."

"Oh?"

Zachary was itching to get away from the embarrassing turn of this conversation.

"Nope. Bramble."

"Pardon?"

"Bram. It's short for Bramble."

Zachary blinked and took in the person before him.

"Your name," he clarified, "is Bramble Larkspur?"

A sober nod.

"Are you perhaps visiting Wyoming from the court of the Fairy Queen?" Zachary blurted.

Bram grinned. Was it a fae grin? Who knew? They could walk among us unobserved—well, unless they went around calling themselves things like *Bramble Larkspur*.

"My parents," Bram said by way of explanation, but trailed off before explaining. "At least I've got a normie nickname. You should meet my siblings." He grinned.

Zachary braced for all kinds of embarrassing names, but as quickly as the grin had come, it was replaced by a soft, fond smile.

"Actually, their names are pretty cool," he said. And he may as well have said *I love them*.

"All right, then, I have to get to work. Good morning, Bramble Larkspur."

For no reason he could account for, Zachary tipped the brim of his hat to his new neighbor. Only he wasn't wearing a hat, so actually he made an awkward movement in front of his own face, almost poked himself in the eye, and dropped his vintage *Fangoria* in the process.

"Damn it," he muttered.

Bram scooped it up before the words had even left his mouth.

"Horror, huh?"

"It's vintage."

Bram raised an eyebrow.

"A collector?"

Zachary squirmed. He needed to get inside if he was going to have time to brew his tea and set up his table to begin work at 8:00 on the dot. But horror movies—and his adjacent collecting—were his favorite topic of conversation.

Bram opened the magazine carefully and began flipping through it. His broad shoulders shook in a shiver and his eyebrows drew together.

"Scary," he said.

"Well. Horror," Zachary replied.

"I'd have nightmares if I watched these kind of movies," Bram said, shivering in the warm morning sun.

"Not all of them are quite as visceral as—" he glanced at the caption under the photograph Bram was looking at "—*Midnight Monster Maul*."

"Still." Bram shook his head. "What do you like about them?"

The words rushed out of Zachary without pause.

"Horror is a genre about extremity. The extremity of the world, of what people do to one another. The extremity of what people are capable of and the extremity of what the human mind can contemplate. It has the power to render perfectly banal household objects terrifying because of their proximity to horror or turn the most harrowing experiences into character-building journeys of strength and self-discovery. It has some of the best scores out there, and artistically it's unrivaled in terms of the expansion of our sense of the body, architecture, creatures, and camera angles. It—"

Zachary caught himself. Bram was looking at him differently now. At first Zachary read it as suspicion, but no. It was…interest?

"Anyway, I really must get to work," he said, and turned on his heel, stiff leather of his brogue digging in unpleasantly.

Zachary closed the door behind him. His heart was beating unusually fast.

Probably Bram was just desperate for company. He'd moved to a street where the only other people under fifty had multiple children, so he probably just saw Zachary as something to keep away the boredom.

But enough thinking about Bram and his shoulders and his biceps and the thickness of his chest. And definitely enough thinking about his blue, blue eyes and the way his hair fell in his face when he bent forward, defying his attempts to rake it back.

Nope. Not thinking about any of those things.

Tea, steeped. Drafting table, adjusted to the perfect height. Score from *The Trouble with Harry*, on. He was ready to begin the day.

The clock clicked over to 8:00.

Chapter Three

Bram

The creature that was emerging from the wood had teeth in unnatural places and wings rising from where wings did not usually rise. It was not a creature of the earth but of the imagination.

And it was all Zachary Glass' fault. Well, his and that damn magazine's.

Bram tossed the carving aside and Hemlock was on it like a shot.

"Go ahead," Bram told her when she paused with it in her mouth, golden eyes looking up pleadingly.

She crunched its wings between her molars, sending the whatever-it-was back to hell.

Bram sighed. He'd never been given to boredom—the world was so damn interesting and there were always things to learn and explore. But he'd also never lived a thousand miles away from all the people he cared about and not had a job before. He groaned. A job. Yeah. He definitely needed to find one, and quick. Not just for the money—six months without paying rent had allowed him to save a comforting chunk of the money from working at the tree farm—but because he liked to have a place he needed to be most days. And it helped him enjoy the time he wasn't working more.

Blargh I need to get a job, Bram texted his older sister, Birch.

you've been there like six minutes, take a breath.

I hate breathing.

snort how is it though?

It's good, I think. Nice people.

uh huh.

What?!

"nice people?" ok stepford wife.

They ARE nice. Well… He thought about Zachary across the street. mostly. They do this Halloween decoration competition every year so I thought maybe I'd participate.

good! That's a great idea. make some friends, make some weird halloween art. perfect.

Bram saw her ellipsis for a long time, then a series of random letters. Then she wrote: oops gtg millie is destroying everything <3 <3

Love you, Bram wrote.

Millie was his niece, and at three years old she was already clearly going to invent an elixir of life or create a humanity-ending bomb. Bram casually crossed his fingers, hoping for the former.

So, with nothing else to do and Birch's encouragement front of mind, he decided he might as well start thinking about what his options were for Halloween decorations.

"Yeah, okay, I'll just… I'll go into town and get some stuff to make…things…"

Hem cocked her head at him as if to say, *What are you going to get? And you don't know where anything is.*

"Well, we'll explore. Wanna come?"

She barked once and Bram held up his hand. She touched her paw to his hand in a high five.

The black-and-brown Triumph Scrambler was the one thing Bram hadn't sold when he left Washington. He and his father had restored it lovingly and painstakingly over several years, and even though he hadn't been able to ride it all the long Wyoming winter, he couldn't bear to part with it. And he was glad of that come spring, because zooming through the mountains, their tops still crowned with snow as he basked in the sunshine, had been amazing.

"Motorcycle?" he asked Hemlock.

She barked again, and Bram got down her harness from the peg inside the door.

She followed him into the garage and when he patted the backpack she stood on her hind legs and let him strap her to his back.

They got all sorts of funny looks on the road, but no way was Bram risking Hem falling off and getting hurt.

He pulled on his helmet and strapped Hem's leather goggles to her head, nuzzling her ears as he did so.

They zoomed down Casper Road, the bike, the dog, and the man, and turned onto Route 25 toward downtown Garnet Run.

Small as it was, the main street (called Main Street) was quaint and boasted two or three dozen stores. Bram parked the bike in a street spot off Main and unstrapped Hem.

"C'mon, girl," he said, unsnapping her leather goggles and exchanging them for a leash.

Hem's tongue still lolled dryly from her mouth and her eyes were wild from the road.

"You speed demon," Bram said affectionately, sticking out his knuckles for her to lick in an attempt to uncross her eyes.

There was a coffee shop, a secondhand clothing store, two art galleries, a handful of restaurants, an ice cream place, and several stores that seemed to deal in Wyoming-specific wares that Bram couldn't quite clock. There was also an antique store, a fabric store, and a movie theater. The marquee announced that the Odeon was currently playing a film called *The Omega Man* that Bram had never heard of, but that weekend the Saturday night showing was part of their classic film series.

"Should I go?" Bram asked Hem.

He'd always preferred making things with his hands

or exploring the outdoors to movies, but this was a new town, and he was a new Bram.

At least, he was trying to be.

He was trying to be a Bram who didn't trust quite so easily. Who didn't miss the signs of disaster that were right under his nose. Who didn't get his heart stomped on by two of the most important people in his life.

So maybe this Bram also liked movies?

"You lost?" came a voice from the front door of the theater.

It was a man dressed in an outfit that seemed from another time. He had red hair combed into an impressive pompadour and had his thumbs hooked in his suspenders.

"Oh, not really. More…getting the lay of the land."

"Sure," the man said. "Let me know if you need any help. I'm the newest arrival to town, so I can tell you where things are using actual street names and miles instead of landmarks you don't know because Mrs. Mankowitz's burned down sixteen years before you arrived."

Bram chuckled and held out his hand.

"Bram Larkspur. Usurping newest arrival."

"Henry Finch," said the redhead, his grip warm and dry, "and I'm very happy to cede the title. Not that it'll do me any good. Or you, for that matter. We'll both be the new arrivals until we die. Just how Garnet Run works."

"Did you say new arrival?" another voice said.

Olympia was a small town, really, and the Larkspurs were known by reputation. You couldn't really be a family of seven living on a mostly-off-the-grid farm without people knowing of you. But it was also the kind of casually chill place where people greeted you with a nod or an eyebrow raise. This sudden hailing of not one but two people in close succession was slightly overwhelming. But, hey, Bram had said he wanted to make friends—maybe this would be the beginning.

Bram turned to find one of the most striking men he'd ever seen ambling toward them, his walk liquid and his eyes almost silver. He had long black hair and sinuous tattoos on most of his visible skin.

"Hey, Rye!" Henry said. "This is… Sorry, I already forgot your name."

"I'm Bram." He held his hand out to Rye.

"Rye Janssen. And what the hell are they putting in the water in Garnet Run, because it seems like the population of hot guys increases every time I turn around. And I am including myself in that comment."

His smile was sharp, and he looked at Bram appreciatively, but it was a casual once-over, and Bram felt only the warmth of friendship from him.

"Just arrived," Bram confirmed. "From Olympia."

He opened his mouth to answer the questions everyone else had asked next, but Rye had already lost interest in him apparently, because he dropped to his heels on the sidewalk and held out a hand for Hem.

"She's gorgeous. What's her name?"

"Hemlock."

Rye grinned. "Dark. I like it."

"Oh, it's a tree…" Bram began, but Rye just winked and said, "Yeah, and a poison."

"So, you mentioned some directions," Bram said to Henry. "I'm looking for a place to get some supplies for Halloween decorations. Apparently this street I just moved to has an annual contest—"

"Oh shit, did you move to Casper Road?" Rye interrupted. "Wicked! I've got to get over there this year and see all the haunted houses."

"It seems fun," Bram offered, though *fun* was not quite the right word.

"Gotta make your own fun here," Rye said. "Or if you're Henry, you make all of our fun."

He nodded to the theater.

"Did you…make this place?" Bram asked.

"I restored it."

"Wow. I thought I might come to the showing on Saturday night. I haven't seen that many movies, but…"

A look of horror flashed on Henry's face before he schooled his expression. "You definitely should come," Henry said.

"Um, anyway, do you know where I could get some things for decorations?"

"What're you looking for?" Rye asked. He smirked at Henry's horror. "My boyfriend owns the hardware store." Rye's face lit up adorably when he said the word *boyfriend*. "So he could hook you up with lumber or tools or paint. But if you want, like, craft stuff, you should totally check out Miss Miriam's." He pointed at the fabric store. "She has the weirdest combination of crafty stuff. Like, bins of multicolored puffs and googly eyeballs and every marker ever made. That kind of thing."

"And if you don't relish picking through a grave-yard of googly eyes," Henry offered, "there's a Michael's in East River, about twenty-five minutes' drive from here."

Bram, who loved to support small business, made a promise to himself that he'd check Miss Miriam's first, even if he had to contend with googly eyes.

"Can you tell me where the hardware store is?" he asked Rye.

"I'll escort you," he said. "I was on my way there anyway."

"Nice to meet you, fellow new arrival," Bram told Henry, and Henry extracted a promise that he'd come to the showing that Saturday, assuring Bram that it would help him love movies.

Rye clapped Henry congenially on the back as they left. The second they were out of sight, though, he said, "Henry is the best and that theater is gorgeous. But some of his movies are booooring." He feigned sleep.

"I've never been the biggest movie fan, but I did just move here, so…"

"Oh, I totally get it," Rye said immediately. "I was the new guy before Henry."

They turned the corner and crossed the street into the parking lot of a store that looked like it was straight out of a mom-and-pop hardware store catalogue. The sign painted in huge letters on the side of the building said Matheson's Hardware and Lumber in green Western font, and when they walked in, a bell cheerfully announced their presence.

The man who approached from behind the counter appeared to have been ordered from the same catalogue as the store itself: he was extremely tall and thick—taller than Bram's own six foot two and broader too. He had a reddish-brown beard and kind eyes, painters' pants with an actual hammer slung through the hammer loop, and worn brown boots. His apron also said Matheson's and his name tag said Charlie.

"Hey, darlin'," Charlie said to Rye, and clapped a huge hand over the other man's shoulder.

Rye lifted his chin and smiled a private smile. Then his edges fell back into place and he turned back to Bram.

"Charlie, this is Bram and Hemlock. Bram just moved here."

"To Garnet Run?" Charlie inquired, voice a warm rumble.

"I know, right? What's up? Did some lonely gay make a deal with the devil to bring all these hotties to town or what?"

Charlie coughed to cover a laugh and held his hand out for Hem to smell.

"From Washington State?" he asked.

Rye's eyes went wide, then he frowned.

"Who told you? Was it Clive? I really thought I had one up on you this time cuz I literally just ran into him on the street."

"I didn't hear from anyone," Charlie said. "But Hemlock is the state tree of Washington, and—" he turned to Bram "—you look like a tree man."

"A lumbersexual, you mean," Rye muttered completely audibly.

Bram explained about Casper Road and the Halloween decorations he hoped to create.

"You'll really have to something spectacular if you want to stand a chance at winning," Charlie explained. "The same person has won for the last six years."

Bram didn't have to ask who it was. He'd already met the prickly, formal, vaguely unfriendly winner in the flesh.

"Zachary Glass."

Chapter Four

Zachary

It had been a week since the new guy moved in. He was an early riser—even earlier than Zachary. By the time Zachary went to pick up the mail at 7:30, he was there. Sitting on the porch whittling as that damn dog snoozed on the steps like jelly poured down the stairs.

And every morning, he raised a hand in welcome as Zachary opened his front door.

Listen, Zachary wasn't antisocial. He liked people! Sometimes. But not when they were always *there*, in the place where he was used to carrying out his routines in peace.

Fine, other people on the street were awake at that time, and sometimes they even said hello. But this was different, because…well, it just was. Those people weren't distracting like Bram. They didn't stick in Zachary's mind like gum in the hair, until excision was necessary. And they didn't look at him like Bram did. In fact, he was noticing that no one had ever looked at him quite like Bram did…

But that wasn't the point. The point was…um…

"Morning," Bram said easily, raising a gloved hand.

Zachary walked deliberately to the mailbox.

"Hello."

Bram rose from his stoop, placed a calming hand on the dog's head, and crossed the street to Zachary.

"So, there is a mystery on Casper Road. It's been eating at me and you're just the person to solve it."

"I am?"

Zachary did love mysteries.

"Yeah. Who is the woman at the end of the street and *what* is up with those piles of rocks and sticks? I walked by the other day and I couldn't tell if it was modern art or something out of that Blair Witch movie. That was a horror movie, right?"

Zachary snorted but couldn't help leaning in, delighted.

"Right? That's Mrs. Lundy. She does them every year for the contest, but, like, would she be doing them anyway? Maybe she lived here and made them for twenty years before the decorating contest began? She's been in that house since the seventies."

Zachary had gleaned that bit of knowledge from Marcy Hannity, but even Marcy—possessed as she seemed to be with an uncanny knowledge of all that went on within the auspices of Casper Road—didn't know anything more about Mrs. Lundy. Or if she did, she wasn't sharing it.

"Well, what does Mrs. Lundy say about them?"
Zachary blinked.

"What?"

Bram's expression was open, and he narrowed his eyes.

"I mean, did you ever ask her?"

"No."

"Come on."

Zachary's body was torn by ambivalence. He only had eleven minutes until it was time to start work and he still needed to make his tea.

But he had been curious about Mrs. Lundy for six years.

"I have to work," he began.

Bram just raised an eyebrow and snapped his fingers behind him. The dog trotted over and licked his hand.

"Your call," Bram said. "You wanna go solve a mystery, Hem?"

The dog yipped and Bram stuffed his whittling gloves in the back pocket of his jeans.

"Later, Zachary."

And he loped off down Casper Road, dog at his side.

Zachary turned to go back inside his house and complete his morning routine. A dynamic morning routine was an integral part of setting up the day for success.

But he snuck one more glance at the man and the pull was so strong he couldn't resist.

"Wait up," he called, and jogged a few steps to walk on Bram's other side.

"Yay," Bram said, like a child whose friend has agreed to go on an adventure.

"So, solve another mystery for me," Bram said.

"What's that?"

"Well, the mail comes at around 4:00 p.m. usually. Why do you get yours the next morning?"

Zachary cringed yet again at the thought that his routine was being so closely observed. See, this was why he didn't like that Bram got up early.

As if he sensed Zachary's irritation, Bram said, "It's none of my business. Sorry. My family always says I'm too nosy." He paused for a few steps and then continued. "I don't *mean* to be nosy, really. I'm just really curious about people. I like to know why different people do different things."

Zachary certainly believed that, given the task they were currently engaged in.

Bram's genuine curiosity was disarming, and Zachary found himself telling the truth.

"I like to have a routine that supports my morning momentum. I've found that going outside is helpful, and I like to have somewhere to go. When there's mail, it gives me something to look forward to because I let myself open it as a reward when I'm done with work for the day."

He set his shoulders, bracing for the inevitable comments. But Bram just nodded, accepting the answer frictionlessly.

Mrs. Lundy's house was the last house on Casper Road—or the first, Zachary supposed. An ugly brick box from the sixties, it looked heavy and boring from the front.

The piles of stones and sticks seemed to appear like magic. Certainly Zachary had never seen Mrs. Lundy constructing them, and he didn't get the sense anyone else had either.

Suddenly, Zachary had the creeping sense that they'd wandered into a horror movie. It would be revealed that there was no Mrs. Lundy. That the piles of stones and sticks birthed themselves on the locations of each person Mrs. Lundy's ghost drained of life force to stay haunting this hideous sixties minimalism.

He giggled at the idea.

"What?" Bram asked, as if he'd welcome the chance to be included in a joke.

"Nothing. Just imagining that this would make a really good start to a horror movie."

"Well, at least I would live," Bram said seriously. "Because I'm a virgin."

Zachary blinked, torn between surprise at Bram's comment and surprise that he knew that trope if he didn't watch horror movies.

The latter was more interesting.

"I thought you didn't watch horror movies?" Zachary asked.

"I might've googled after your impassioned speech."

Zachary was touched.

"It's interesting. Maybe we could watch one sometime and you can tell me about all the tropes. But *not* a super-scary one," he said intently.

This had taken an unexpected turn and he didn't know what to think about it.

"We could do that," Zachary murmured.

From the lace-swathed front window a voice issued, startling them both.

"Are you boys going to stand there casing the joint or are you going to knock on my door?"

Zachary's mouth fell open.

"Mrs. Lundy," he whispered to Bram, as if confronted with a celebrity or a ghost.

"Get over here," she said, and the front door swung open.

Zachary wished he could say it creaked or that her voice sounded like wind rushing through a graveyard, or *something* picturesque. But the front door swung open just fine and Mrs. Lundy's voice was surprisingly youthful.

"Let me guess," she said, still in the shadows. "You've come to tell me I won the lottery."

Zachary smiled but a look of horror crossed Bram's face.

"Oh no. No, ma'am, I'm so sorry. That's not—"

"Don't hurt yourself, young man. That was a joke."

Bram turned red and spluttered. Zachary had never liked him more.

"Would you like to come in?"

Mrs. Lundy stepped into the light.

If it had been a horror movie, she would have been a beautiful siren, intent on luring them inside to their doom (horror movies were often disappointingly heterosexual). Or a meek-looking old woman with murder in her eyes.

But this was not a horror movie, and Mrs. Lundy just looked kind of like Bea Arthur. She wore neatly pressed blue slacks and a green button-down shirt that hung loose at the shoulders and was rolled up to her elbows. She had half-moon glasses on a cord around her neck, and her white hair was cut into the nondescript short style that so many women over the age of sixty-five eventually got.

Her eyes were not murderous. But they were notable. A bright, piercing blue, they were so intense that Zachary felt like she could see through his clothes, his skin, to the very beating heart of him.

Though god knew why she would want to.

"Well?" she said, and Zachary realized they'd both stood there staring at her for the better part of thirty seconds. Which, it turned out, was quite long in the realm of amounts-of-time-it's-not-awkward-to-stare-at-strangers.

"Yes, please," Bram said. "Should I leave Hemlock out here?"

Zachary could practically see the joke on the tip of Mrs. Lundy's tongue and the moment she swallowed it, likely remembering how well the last one had gone over.

"No, that's fine. I enjoy dogs."

They trooped inside and Zachary blinked. He was standing in a structure he recognized. Could it really be?

A stunned sound made its way out of his throat and Bram put a hand on his shoulder as if he were choking.

"Is this… Is this a McTeague?"

Mrs. Lundy's eyes sparked.

"Well done. It is."

Norris McTeague's houses were the architectural version of the shot in *Blue Velvet* where the camera descended beneath a perfectly manicured suburban front lawn to show the writhe of insects underneath. Walls that would usually create privacy were just wood framing covered with acrylic sheeting—transparent but unable to be passed through. In other places where there were solid walls, the material was sandwiched between more acrylic sheeting, suggesting you should be able to see through it but could not.

"Holy bananas," Zachary muttered, something his mother used to say when she didn't want to swear around children. He didn't know where it came from, only that it was accompanied by an unfamiliar pang of longing for his mother, whom he hadn't seen in over two years. They spoke every now and then on the phone, but only briefly.

"Are you an admirer of McTeague's, or a detractor?" Mrs. Lundy asked.

Admirers said his houses were a play of opacity and transparency, privacy and exposure. The acrylic walls had no way to hang art or mirrors, turning the views of or through them into art or entertainment. By placing someone else in another room that you could see into, they became unreachable but also watchable, like a character in a painting or film. They were a meditation on what parts of the home were valued, were public, were private, and they upended the hierarchy of a house that was finished over one that was being built or falling apart, making us question what *finished* even meant.

Detractors said his constructions were abominations, turning the home, where one should feel comfortable and in control, into bizarre aquaria in which family members gawked at one another. They were alienating, dehumanizing, and borderline terrifying. Zachary always thought of McTeague when he watched haunted house movies. They too turned the home into a site of fear and uncertainty rather than comfort.

"Oh, an admirer. That is, I admire all the things he experimented with, but I don't *like* his work, aesthetically. Uh, no offense intended," he added, realizing he'd essentially insulted her home.

"None received. Can I offer you something?" Mrs. Lundy said politely. "While you tell me why you were lingering outside my house."

"Oh, no thank you," Bram said, at the same time Zachary said, "We wanted to know what the deal is with the sticks and stones."

Mrs. Lundy raised an eyebrow at him as if he'd confirmed her suspicions, and gestured them to follow her.

In the living room, Zachary marveled at the design typical of a McTeague. Half the wall into the kitchen was just framing and acrylic sheeting, so you'd be able to watch someone appear as if they were entering a stage from the wings. The other half showed the exposed framing and insulation of the wall. The ceiling was hammered tin panels, except for a cutout in the center that created a window to the second floor. The effect was truly unique.

"What do you think of them?" she asked, sitting on an armchair. Zachary and Bram sat on the love seat, the only other place to sit in the room, and immediately fell into each other as their weight sagged them both to the middle of the cushion.

Bram's shoulder was warm and solid against Zachary's.

"I think they're wonderful," Bram said.

"Undeniably," Zachary said. "What do they mean?"

"I don't want to shock you," Mrs. Lundy said.

Bram and Zachary leaned in. Bram smelled like wood shavings and sunshine and something sweet like peaches.

Mrs. Lundy leaned in too.

"They're how I communicate with my home planet."

Zachary's heart fell. Mrs. Lundy wasn't an artist or a witchy crone. She was an old, mentally ill woman without a support network.

Bram seemed, for the first time, to have nothing to say in response to that either, and the silence grew uncomfortable.

"Oh good lord, I'm just kidding. I swear, your generation has no sense of humor at all."

Zachary's mouth fell open.

"Also no manners. What are your names?"

"Oh jeez, so sorry." Bram stood and held out his hand. "I'm Bram Larkspur, recently arrived to Casper Road. Lovely to meet you."

"Zachary Glass," Zachary said.

"Imelda Lundy," she said, inclining her head graciously. "Lovely to make your acquaintance. Now. I'm afraid I'll have to disappoint you. I don't come from another planet. And I wasn't an enfant terrible in the New York art scene. Nor am I an evil witch who dines on the flesh of children who wander onto my property and uses their bones in her autumn sculptures. Alas."

"Seriously," Zachary muttered. That would be an awesome contemporary retelling of Hansel and Gretel. Way better than the horrible 2015 remake.

"What are you, then?" Zachary asked. "I mean, what are *they*?"

"I grew up here. Garnet Run. When I was a little girl, my father was a hunter. He made piles of stones—

or, when there weren't stones, sticks—to mark his path, to measure rising or falling water levels in streams he needed to cross, to mark a campsite he wished to return to for the night. Sometimes to communicate with other hunters or trappers."

Mrs. Lundy's eyes took on a faraway look.

"He used to bring me home a stone each time he returned from a hunt. Stones worn smooth by the river. I painted on them. Drew faces."

She smiled.

"When Marcy Hannity first proposed the idea of a Casper Road Halloween decoration corridor and asked me to participate, I found myself out in the yard, stacking stones. I think they're beautiful. And I'm certainly not going to spend my money on a lot of plastic decorations at Walmart."

Zachary winced at her mention of the hated place.

"You'd know all about that, Zachary Glass, six-time winner of the Casper Road Halloween Decorating Contest."

"You know who I am?"

"Of course. You don't miss a young man who works from home dressed in a suit all year-round. And I've certainly appreciated your compelling approach to the holiday."

Zachary glowed with her praise.

"Thank you."

"I assume you'll be starting to decorate soon?"

Zachary's stomach knotted. He was behind in his planning and his execution. Work had been unusually busy the last two months. He should really catch up this weekend. He had a title to defend.

"Yes, very soon," he said coolly.

But the joy of solving the mystery of Mrs. Lundy's sculptures was swiftly giving way to the anxiety of starting work late. He really needed to get home.

Chapter Five

Bram

The chainsaw screamed and Bram winced.

"Can I give you a hand there, Carl?"

The older man was sweating and heaving. Bram moved behind him and pulled the cord to turn off the saw, then took it out of his hands.

"I borrowed this from my brother. He never uses it. Just wanted to clear this stump."

"I got it," Bram said, and went to work on the stubborn wood.

Twenty minutes later, he'd excised the stump and was working on the roots.

"Thank you so much," Carl said. "I thought I was gonna chop my leg off or something."

"It's not great to use a chainsaw with no training,"

Bram said gently. He forbore from telling Carl that he'd seen someone drop a chainsaw on their foot and the cuts the rotating blade made were nothing so clean as chopping. "What are you going to do with the wood?" Bram asked instead.

"Nothing, just put it out for trash pickup."

"Any chance your brother wouldn't miss this for the weekend?"

"Oh, he won't. He told me to take it for as long as I needed."

"Well then, I know just what to do with the stump."

The first time Bram had carved with a chainsaw had been five years ago, at his sister Moon's woodshop. Chainsaw carving was like whittling on steroids and Bram had enjoyed it immediately, even though it left his shoulders and back aching and his hands with the juddering sense of vibration long after the tool was turned off.

And this was the perfect chance to put those skills to work.

Hem slunk off to lie at the side of the house—she did not appreciate the sound of the chainsaw—as Bram and Carl pulled, rolled, and kicked the heavy stump over to Bram's lawn. It felt so good to do something with his hands. To feel the sweat of exertion along his spine and at his hairline. It never felt like work, using his body. It felt like freedom.

With whittling, the form was all contained within your hand. But this was a much larger project—the stump was nearly as tall as Bram. At first, he circled it, hoping the form would reveal itself. A witch? But Bram didn't like the idea of witches being associated with Halloween. Magic and femininity weren't scary—they were simply oppressed. No witches, then. He ran his fingers along the contours of the stump. It didn't seem rotten, but you never knew what you'd find at the heart of the wood.

Bram had learned recently that the same was true of people.

When he got a sense of the shape, it was obvious. Bram double-checked that the chainsaw cord was knotted to the extension cord, that his hair was tied back. And that his goggles were on. Then he pulled the cord, and the whirring blade touched the wood—a permanent first kiss.

"Oh, damn, that looks good," Moon said. Bram had FaceTimed her to show her the sculpture. "Why a vampire, though?"

He told her about the Casper Road Halloween Decorating Contest and she laughed.

"What, it's fun!" he insisted.

"Yeah, totally. I'm laughing at the idea of you being in a contest. Mr. Can't-we-just-call-it-a-tie when you won that ropes course thing in high school."

Bram smiled. It was true: he'd never cared for competition. He didn't see the value in investing in someone else's outcome over your own. Winning and losing didn't mean anything except the relative caliber of the competition. True valuable competition was always with yourself: how well were you doing compared to how well you could do. Nothing else really mattered.

"You weren't complaining then," he said. "When you would've lost." Yeah, competition didn't matter. But you never missed an opportunity to trash-talk a sibling.

"Yeah, yeah, yeah," Moon said good-naturedly. "So tell me what else is going on."

He chatted with Moon for ten minutes or so, filling her in on the charms of Garnet Run.

As he was telling her about downtown, the Odeon, and the hardware store, and his meeting with Mrs. Lundy (whom he'd made a standing weekly tea date with and whom he wasn't completely convinced had been joking about using her sculptures to communicate with her home planet), the shade in Zachary Glass' front window rose, and then the door opened. It must have been 6:00 p.m.

Zachary strode down the driveway and crossed to Bram.

"What is that?" he demanded, pointing at the sculpture.

"Aw, you can't tell?"

Bram was a bit disappointed; he really thought he'd nailed the cape and the classic widow's peak/fang combo.

"It is an enormous vampire carved out of a tree trunk," Zachary confirmed, and Bram's heart lifted. "I meant, *what* is it doing here?"

Zachary's dark eyes burned with anger.

"It's…a Halloween decoration?" Bram said, not sure where the anger was coming from.

Maybe it had been foolish, but part of his motivation behind doing the sculpture was that he thought Zachary would be pleased—he seemed so invested in the Halloween decorations on Casper Road and he loved horror movies. Surely he was a vampire fan?

"Listen," Zachary said, drawing himself up and squaring his shoulders. He was a small guy, but he certainly had presence. His narrowed eyes were fixed on Bram's face and when he spoke his voice dripped with poison. He was the opposite of the excited, curious, awed man who had visited Mrs. Lundy with Bram the other day.

"I have won this competition for the last six years and I *will* win it again this year. I don't care if you carve every Hammer monster in the world, my decorations have a *concept* and are *highly complex* in execution. So just..." He seemed to have run out of words, but not of anger. "Just don't you forget it!" he concluded, with a finger jab in Bram's direction for emphasis. It was a ridiculous threat and Zachary seemed to be aware of its absurdity as he winced, but he also clearly meant it. He turned on the heel of his fancy, uncomfortable-looking shoes, and stalked back inside.

Bram stood, deflated. Suddenly the vampire didn't look so great. It was just a hunk of wood that made Zachary upset.

"OY, BRAMBLE, HELLO!!"

He'd forgotten Moon was still on FaceTime. "Sorry." He lifted his phone hand from his side.

"Was that your neighbor?" Moon asked.

Bram nodded miserably and regarded the vampire. "Think I should chop his head off and dispatch him?"

"First of all, you stake vampires, not chop their heads off. Second of all, abso-freaking-lutely *not*. That pompous ass needs to be taken *down*."

Bram laughed. Moon always cheered him up.

"No, I'm serious. You're new in town, you don't have a job, and you're all messed up and broken-hearted."

"Thanks for the reminder," he grumbled.

"What else have you got in your life but *grinding this guy into the ground*?!"

"Didn't we *just* agree that competition isn't really my thing?"

"Bramble Aaron Larkspur. There is a time and a place for playing to your strengths and there is a time and place for doing something awesome! You need to take that guy down! I mean, have fun too, obviously. But you love making shit. Just make shit to win."

"Make shit to win, the Moon Larkspur motto."

"Ha-ha. And yes. So, what's the plan?"

"I don't…have one? Because you just told me to do this five seconds ago."

"Yah I know. Let's go make a plan!"

"Now?"

"What, you got something better to do?"

He really, really did not.

"That's what I thought. Hey, before we go in, point me toward that asshole."

Bram rolled his eyes and pointed his phone screen across the street, confident that the sound would not carry.

"It is on!" Moon yelled. *"It is so, so on!"*

Bram was having fun. Actual fun, not "my heart is broken and I am destroyed but ha-ha isn't this a blast" fun like he had been having for the last six months.

He and Moon had spent hours on the phone the week before planning out his decorations. They'd conferenced Thistle and Vega into the call, of course, and Vega had texted Birch and their dad, and before long they all just moved to Skype for the rest of the planning session. Each Larkspur had, upon getting the gloss from Moon about what they were doing, said some version of "*Bram* is entering a competition??" And Birch had nodded in agreement every single time.

Which was nice, because his family knew him. But also made him think that maybe it was time to put a little competitive muscle behind this thing. If everyone thought he couldn't do it, he'd love to prove them wrong.

He'd ended the call by thanking them and saying, "I'll win it for you!" Which he thought he'd seen someone say, impassionedly, in a sports movie once. It had seemed the kind of thing you said to the family who helped you. His dad had given him a virtual fist bump and his siblings had dissolved into laughter as he hung up the call. But it had felt so good to be around them, to have them on his side. Besides, they'd had some great ideas.

In fact, he was in the midst of working on one of Thistle's ideas this morning, and he went to the hardware store for supplies.

"Hello," Charlie, the owner, said brightly when he walked in. "Bram, right?"

"Yeah."

They shook hands and Bram described what he needed to Charlie, unfolding a sketch he'd done of it and flattening it on the counter.

"Whoa! Is that a dragon?"

That was the comment from a sweet-looking blond guy behind the counter.

"It's supposed to be, yeah. A fire-breathing dragon. I'll put the light in here." He tapped the drawing. "Then the shadows should fall like this" He drew the shapes of fangs that should fall over the lawn from another light behind the piece.

"And you're going to carve this. With a chainsaw."

"Yep." Bram grinned as the blond man's eyebrows disappeared under his messy bangs. He reached out a hand and placed it over the drawing, as if to cover it from anyone's eyes.

"Listen," the man said intently, looking around. "I need you to swear that you will never—and I mean *never*—tell my daughter that you can carve sculptures with a chainsaw. Because my insurance is not good enough for that. No offense, boss," he added to Charlie.

Charlie shook his head somberly. "I really wish I could offer better insurance," he said. "I'm working on it with some other businesses—"

"Charlie, I know! Don't worry. Not my point."

"Okay," Bram assured him. "I don't know your daughter, but I promise I'll never tell her about chainsaw carving?"

A little girl with the same blond hair skipped out from the back room.

"What's chainsaw carving?" she asked intently.

The blond man froze, and Charlie started coughing spasmodically.

"Math," Bram tossed out casually, then kept talking as he had been. "Anyway, I think I need to source the lumber from someplace indoors. Moisture content in the wood, you know?"

The little girl looked disappointed and wandered back into the bowels of the store.

"Bless you," the blond man said and there was sincere relief in his face. "It's just that I'm still not over the tarantula phase and I don't think I can take the constant threat of grievous bodily harm. Oh, I'm Adam, by the way. And she's Gus."

Bram laughed. "No problem. Bram." Then the sense of familiarity clicked. "I think I sold you and your daughter a Christmas tree last year."

Adam flushed. "Yup, you did."

"He's the one who told me about Garnet Run!" Bram said to Charlie, realization dawning.

Charlie just smiled.

Charlie knew just who to get the wood from—Charlie seemed to know just where and from whom to get everything in Garnet Run—and offered to lend Bram his truck since Bram certainly couldn't transport tree trunks on a motorcycle.

"That would be so great. I really appreciate it. Let me know if you want a carving for outside your shop."

Charlie's eyes twinkled.

"You know what. I know just who would want one."

Which is how Bram found himself outside someplace called the Dirt Road Cat Shelter.

Rye, the man he'd met the week before and Charlie's partner, opened the door.

"Did I hear Charlie right on the phone? You could do a *chainsaw* carving of a *cat* out of a *tree trunk*??"

"Well, yeah. I mean, I've never done a cat before, so I can't guarantee the realism. Cats are kind of smooth curves and, well, it's a chainsaw. But, yeah, basically."

"I am so damn glad you moved here," Rye said sincerely.

Chapter Six

Zachary

Zachary was behind. It was September 1st. Usually by this time, he'd have his armatures created, his lighting scheme signed off on by Wes, his best friend, and be spending a satisfying Saturday night in his studio, movies playing, ideas firing, as he painted, papier-mâchéd, et cetera. He *had* a concept, but not the time to bring it to life.

Instead, he was hunched over his drafting table long after he should've been done with work for the day, scrubbing out lines with an already overworked eraser. This project was a disaster, and it was his fault. Darcy, his closest collaborator/competition at work, had told him from the beginning that the partners weren't going to respond well to something this innovative. That they were looking for clean, obvious design. And Zachary knew she was right.

But there was something in him that had pushed. Had whispered that *this time* was *the* time. The time to show them that he was so much more than box stores and condominiums. More than simple and functional. That he, Zachary Glass, was visionary.

The design he pitched had been lovely and interesting and, as the partners had immediately told him, expensive. And that was what it all boiled down to: innovation was worth less than the money they'd have to spend to make it a reality. It was so damned depressing Zachary could scream.

There had been a time when architecture was art. When the shapes of the spaces people moved through spoke of vision, of the future. Pushed boundaries. Asked questions. Made people pay attention to the world around them.

Even Zachary wasn't so egotistical as to imagine himself creating the next Notre Dame, the next Mosque of Samarra. But even Mrs. Lundy's house had vision. McTeague had sparked controversy in the fifties and sixties. It was ugly, to Zachary and to many others, but who cared?! It was visionary! It changed the way people thought about their own living spaces— insisted they confront the concept of *home* as much as his designs themselves. And it laid the groundwork for what would become industrialism later on.

Zachary sighed and allowed himself ten minutes to feel sorry for himself. He texted Wes: My bosses are visionless hacks. I am deeply misunderstood. Cry for me, Argentina.

Your bosses ARE visionless hacks, Wes replied. They weren't into the gator?

Seeing it in text, it had perhaps been a mistake to call the development Gator. But the Florida mall had four anchor points, a curving tail of a movie theater, and second stories on one half that made its head and chest rear up from the water of the parking lots that surrounded it. Not that you could tell that with a casual glance, but concepts mattered!

Well, not now, since the design would never see the light of day.

You need to be somewhere that lets you have more freedom, Wes wrote.

This made complete sense coming from Wes, who worked on his own, for himself, and only cared about the results. But Zachary *liked* structure. He liked order, and predictability, and having other people tell him he was doing a good job. He liked the competition of vying for the next project with his coworkers. Besides, unlike Wes, Zachary didn't have a large savings account to fall back on.

Nope, Zachary would just take the next three minutes, now, and finish feeling sorry for himself, and then he'd redo the design the way the partners wanted. The Gator would stay in the swamp and he'd produce a safe, boring, *cheap* building full of ninety-degree angles, ceilings the height of premanufactured beams, and no windows so that shoppers couldn't be reminded that there was a world outside the mall.

With a self-indulgent sigh and head full of numbers, Zachary slid a fresh sheet of paper onto the table and began to design Florida's most boring mall. And if something inside him died a little every time he abandoned one of his own designs like this, well. That was life, wasn't it.

Bram Larkspur had to be stopped.

Zachary had woken up Sunday morning, exhausted from his redesign the night before, but excited to spend the day on his Halloween decorations. Even though he was behind by his own standards, he was still light-years ahead of everyone but Mrs. Lundy (fortunately though regrettably not a threat).

But when he looked out the window, his heart skipped a beat and his stomach clenched. Sprawling across Bram Larkspur's front yard was a-a-a *beast*. A terrifying and glorious dragon creature with a tail that curled to a wicked point and a body that rose eight or nine feet tall. The head then dipped down, like it could peer at anyone who passed. It seemed to be carved out of five different tree stumps of varying heights and sizes that fit artfully together.

It was magnificent.

It was stunning.

And Zachary could feel his victory slipping away. He closed the shade quickly, unable to look at it—or the man who'd created it—for one more second. He didn't get Saturday's mail on Sundays, so he'd have something to get on Monday mornings as part of his routine, so there was no need to leave the house.

He needed to rethink his Halloween plans, find places where he could turn up the volume, because this? This was a shot fired across the bow and Zachary was sure as hell going to return fire.

Three hours later and Zachary's stomach was in

knots. He loved his design of a ghost ship cutting through dark, monster-infested waters! He'd been working on it since late November, and it was perfect. He didn't want to change it. But he couldn't trust the committee to make the right choice.

Zachary paced around the house manically. He had already compromised his last three designs for the firm, and he'd be damned if he was going to do it for his own Halloween decorations. Why did Bram have to come here?

He was ruining *everything*.

Zachary didn't precisely *mean* to do it. But before he knew what he was doing, he had grabbed a tin of yellow paint left over from the previous year's design in his hand, and was stalking across the street.

Up close, the dragon was even more amazing. Zachary snarled at it and it snarled back. But since it was just wood, it couldn't stop him when he tossed the can of sunshine yellow paint all over it.

As paint hit wood, Zachary felt a moment of spiteful elation. But in the second after, when the beautiful sculpture dripped paint onto the grass, Zachary felt light-headed.

"Oh my god, oh my god, oh god, *shit*!"

That's when he saw something move behind the window of Bram's house—something tall and Bram-shaped. He'd been seen. He stood frozen for a moment, wondering what he could do, but there was nothing to do. So he turned and ran back to his house, shut the door behind him like he'd been running from an ax murderer, and closed his eyes.

This was low. This was so low. He couldn't believe he'd done something so mean, so destructive, so incredibly petty. And to someone who'd just moved to town and didn't know anyone.

Zachary barely made it to the bathroom before puking.

Chapter Seven

Bram

"**D**id you just…" Bram goggled as he watched through the window as Zachary Glass splashed paint on his dragon creature. At first, Bram had thought it was silly string, something he and his siblings used to spray on each other's belongings as a prank. But one look at Zachary's face in the moment after he doused the dragon disabused him of that notion.

And he'd kind of thought they were becoming friendly. Unless…maybe Zachary meant it in a friendly way? *No! God, stop giving everyone the benefit of the doubt when they're obviously being an asshole*, he heard his sister Moon say.

But the truth was that Bram had begun to *enjoy* Zachary. He wasn't quite sure why yet. The man was snarky, uptight, and borderline rude, didn't seem to have a sense of humor, and dressed like he was on *Mad Men*. But there was just something about him that drew Bram in. He was intense and passionate, unapologetic and very straightforward.

Well, if you didn't count the fact that he was currently scurrying from the scene of the crime.

Bram had a choice. You always had a choice. He could choose anger and confront or resent Zachary for what he did. Or he could decide that Zachary's act was a prank. A mean prank, but a prank nonetheless. And Bram could respond in kind.

He chose the latter, and he called in his family for backup.

Chapter Eight

Zachary

Monday morning it was all Zachary could do to open his front door, but he couldn't start his workday without going through his routine. He kept his eyes on the ground, as if maybe that meant he wouldn't see Bram sitting on his stoop behind the paint-splattered dragon.

He would just apologize. Right. He took a deep breath.

"Morning, neighbor," Bram called. His voice was cheery and open.

What the hell? Why would Bram be nice to him when he'd been so awful? Was it possible that it wasn't Bram he'd seen through the window? That Bram didn't know it was him? No, surely not. He'd *seen* Bram see him.

"Um. Morning," Zachary got out, trying to figure out what was wrong with this sunny man. He opened the mailbox absently and reached inside. There should be an issue of *Global Architecture*. But the moment the mailbox opened, something hit him in the face. Shocked, he reeled backward. Had a bomb gone off? Had the world finally ended?

He sputtered and opened his eyes. His mailbox, the ground around it, and presumably he himself, were covered in…glitter?

"What the…?"

"Game on," said a voice over his shoulder, and Zachary turned to see Bram standing there, grinning.

"You—I—Did you—?"

"You started it," Bram said, nodding toward the dragon. "But now it's on."

Zachary goggled. Bram had seen him. He'd seen him do something mean-spirited and awful, and had seen it in the context of a prank…he was either very generous or *very* deluded. And for some reason, Zachary found himself hoping it was the former.

"I'm very, very sorry about the paint. I honestly don't know what possessed me. That is, I wasn't *actually* possessed; I take responsibility for my actions. Just, I didn't actually think I was going to do it until I did, and then, uh, it was too late. Because I'd done it."

"Yeah, that's usually how that works," Bram agreed. But he still didn't seem angry. He seemed…impish.

"Are you…enjoying this?"

Bram just raised his eyebrows and winked. "Consider us even. For now." Then he took a magazine from his back pocket and handed it to Zachary. *Global Architecture*.

"Thanks."

Bram smiled mysteriously and said, "You never

know what I might do next." Then he sauntered back across the street, leaving Zachary a mess of uncertainty and glitter.

When he got a glimpse of himself in the bathroom mirror, he gaped. The glitter coated his skin, his hair, his eyebrows, everything. He looked like some kind of science fiction extra from Planet Sparkle. His mind whirled with ideas, the sick feeling of guilt replaced by something buoyant.

It was eight minutes until he was supposed to start work and now he had to shower again. He was definitely going to get a late start, which usually filled him with irritation and anxiety.

So why was his reflection grinning back at him?

In the shower as he scrubbed the stubborn glitter from his skin, he realized what it was.

He was having fun. And he couldn't remember the last time he had.

Sure, he enjoyed a lot of what he did. He loved designing his buildings, horror movies, corresponding with his pen pals, creating his Halloween decoration-scape. But enjoyment wasn't the same thing as the fizzy joy of pure, shared fun.

Operation Prank War was now Zachary's prime objective and he texted Wes an SOS: I need ideas for pranks. Now that you have a human child, make her say some silly, childish things that I can implement.

Roger that.

While he waited for Wes' boyfriend's daughter Gus' nine-year-old input, Zachary googled "prank." *A prac-*

tical joke or mischievous act. That wasn't very illuminating.

Nor were the pranks listed very useful. They seemed mainly to involve the replacement of one object with another and to require proximity—a shared bathroom that would allow you to replace toothpaste with frosting or shampoo with mayonnaise (disgusting; he would never).

The other kind of pranks were elaborate and seemed to have as their goal the complete destruction of the recipient's sanity. He read about a prank where a suite of college roommates drywalled over the doorway to one of their roommates' bedrooms while he was away for the weekend, and when he returned they all pretended not to know who he was.

That was very impressive, and Zachary filed it away for future use on Wes, if the situation ever arose, but it wasn't right for Bram. Bram was…sunnier. Lighter. For Bram he wanted something, well, fun.

Timing was the soul of comedy, and so Zachary waited for the perfect moment to unleash his find. It came four days later, when a thunderstorm prevented Bram and Hemlock from their daily outdoor whittling (Bram) and lying like a pile of jelly (Hemlock).

When the next morning dawned, Zachary had set it all up. He left his house early and by the back door, and crept around the cul-de-sac, to the side of Bram's house where the inflatable was plugged into the exterior socket. He flipped the switch and watched as the inflatable ghost engorged. It was ten feet tall, and Zachary had situated it directly in front of Bram's front door. When it was fully inflated, Zachary waited.

Bram should be coming outside any minute.

Zachary's fingers were restless, and he was bouncing on the balls of his feet, psychically urging Bram to emerge. Irritatingly, Bram didn't come out at the exact same time every day—didn't, in fact, seem to have any dependable schedule at all. Zachary didn't know how he did it.

After what felt like an age but was only ten minutes, the door began to open. Unfortunately, Zachary couldn't see Bram's face because Bram was inside the house, but he heard his gasp, and he certainly heard Hemlock's low, urgent growl.

Then Bram pushed his way outside past the inflated ghost, a smile on his face. Hemlock sniffed at it in all directions, finally seeming to decide it was no threat, even if it was on her preferred snoozing stoop.

Bram's eyes met Zachary's and they both grinned.

"Nice ghost."

"Thanks."

"What's the law about claiming objects on your property in this state? Is the ghost mine now?"

Uncharacteristically, Zachary had not considered that.

"Do you want it?"

"Yeah! I'll make it part of my Halloween display. Or did you forget about that part?" he mused exaggeratedly.

"Ha-ha."

They stood staring at each other, huge inflatable ghost waving ghostily in the background. Zachary didn't know what to say now. He had loved being the one to put that impish grin on Bram's face. He knew that much.

"So, do you get the ideas for your award-winning decorations from horror movies?" Bram asked.

"Not directly. But certainly their aesthetics have influenced my own. A lot of people think horror is all dark alleys and red blood and, like, black leather torture implements. But there is a huge amount of variation within the genre—and subgenres—everything from super-saturated psychedelic color, to muted and desolate landscapes, to the sunny, bucolic scenes of folk horror."

Bram was listening closely, blue eyes locked on Zachary.

"Which do you like the best?"

"I like all of them in their own ways, really. But do like the subtle and muted palettes. There's something so beautiful and mournful about them. Like…like a field of wild grasses at the start of autumn. All different tones of green and brown and gray and gold."

"Sounds beautiful," Bram murmured. "But not very scary."

"Well, that's the thing about horror. Every scary thing is scary either because it's alien to what we know or because it's the same as what we know. So something could be scary because a field of lovely wild grass looks calm and bucolic and then *BAM*, a monster slinks out of it. But it could also be scary because the grass looks calm and bucolic and then slowly you realize that it's razor sharp and can cut you to ribbons. Or it's stealthily twining around your ankles to keep you in the field forever."

Bram shuddered.

"Those are *all* terrifying. I honestly don't understand how you can watch that stuff."

"Well, those aren't real examples. Although, *Children of the Corn* does take place in a corn field."

"Yeah, I just can't really understand choosing to be scared or anxious. No judgment, honestly, I'm just curious. Why do you like being scared?"

It was something everyone who didn't like horror asked, and Zachary never had a satisfactory answer for them. Taste was just different. But Bram seemed to genuinely want to understand.

"Why do you watch a movie or read a book?"

"Er, I don't that much, honestly. I know that's not cool to admit, but…" He shrugged.

"It's not really about wanting to be scared for me. Sure there are some people who watch horror movies like eating ghost peppers, to prove that they can take it, and the scarier the better. But that's not me. I just… I accept that negative emotions are a part of life, I guess. And horror is a genre that also accepts that. So you get movies where the characters face extreme challenges or threats and are transformed by them, if they survive. People try to push away the bad things. That's what we're taught to do. Bury the dead far away from where we live, say you're fine even if you're having a horrible day, don't think bad thoughts. It's practically superstition. But I think the people who avoid seeing or thinking about scary stuff the most are actually the most affected by it. They believe that even thinking about it has the power to bring it into being. It's almost worshipful."

"I do that," Bram said. "I never thought of it like that, but I totally try and shy away from bad thoughts whenever they come into my head."

"I'm not saying we should like *bathe* in horrors

or anything. But I do think refusing to even think of something gives it more power than it should have."

Bram seemed to think about this for a minute, then screwed up his face.

"Seriously, though, don't you get scared?! It's just so...*scary*."

Zachary smiled.

"So's riding a motorcycle, isn't it."

"Well. I guess...yeah, at first."

"But you like it."

"It's exhilarating. I feel free when I'm on it."

"For me, the more horror I watch, the less scared I am. Like exposure therapy, maybe? My best friend, Wes, has a tarantula and snakes and lizards for pets. He loves them, thinks they're adorable. But his boyfriend has always been terrified of tarantulas. So when they started dating, Adam would hardly even go inside Wes' house when Bettie was around—that's the tarantula. But Adam's daughter, Gus, loved Bettie, and after a while, Adam was around her more and more and he started to feel differently."

"He's not scared anymore?"

"Well, it's a work in progress. It hasn't been that long. But he's definitely less scared now than he used to be. Avoiding our fears just builds them up in our minds and invests them with more power."

"Hmm," Bram rumbled, rubbing his chin. "I still think I'd be scared."

Zachary shrugged. "That's okay. It's not for everyone."

"Yeah, but..." Bram scraped his heel along the ground. "I kinda want to watch one with you. You've got me all curious."

"You weren't scared by being trapped in your house

by a huge ghost," Zachary pointed out, elbowing the inflatable. "Maybe you're not exactly what you think."

A slow smile spread across Bram's lips and he nodded. "Yeah. Maybe I'm not."

"Okay, well." Zachary checked his watch. "Gotta get to work. Bye."

Bram just kept smiling, a warm, appreciative smile that Zachary almost—*almost*—let himself hope might be *for* him and not just because of what he'd done.

Chapter Nine

Bram

"You know," Rye Janssen said, "You could one hundred percent sell these for a shitload of money."

The chainsaw carving of the cat now stood outside the front doors of the Dirt Road Cat Shelter, looking both regal and playful—exactly what Bram had been going for.

He'd returned Carl's brother's chainsaw and borrowed this one from Charlie Matheson's hardware store to do the carving for Rye.

"You think?"

"Um, hell yes. People would pay so much money for this kinda thing if you marketed it right. You could take commissions and deliver them, or sell premades. Both. Whatever you want."

"I don't know if I'm good enough yet. I only just started."

Rye glared and rolled his eyes. "You're good enough, shut up."

Bram laughed. "Thanks. Maybe."

He loved working with his hands. He loved making things. But he craved being useful, and he didn't know if these really fit the bill.

"Do you do other carpentry?" Rye asked.

"Oh yeah. If you can do it with wood, I've done it," he said.

He flushed when Rye raised an expressive eyebrow and said, "Do tell, sailor. I couldn't pay you that much, so feel free to tell me to screw off, but I have a project I wanted to do this winter. I was gonna get Charlie to help me but he's already so busy."

"Okay, what is it?"

"I want to build cat shelters that we could put around town and in the woods. There are cats who don't want to be indoor cats. I already started a catch-neuter-release program for them so there wouldn't be so many kittens getting born. But even though they don't want to be indoor cats, it gets *so* damn cold here in the winter, and they need shelters. Any interest in building some?"

"Yes," Bram said instantly. "I'm in. Just tell me what you need."

Rye snorted. "I didn't even tell you what I could pay you yet."

"Oh right, well. Whatever."

"Great, that's precisely my budget. Charlie already said he'd donate the wood and that I could use the tools in his shop. So really what I need is like a sketch or something, so I know how much wood to get him to order."

"No problem. How many do you want?"

"Let's start with twenty and then we'll see?"

"On it," Bram said, and he left smiling, thrilled to have a way to help.

That night, he knocked on number 666 Casper Road. It was the first time he'd gotten any closer than Zachary's mailbox and he found himself expecting, for a moment, a giant ax blade to swing down between himself and the front door. That was how remote and inaccessible Zachary sometimes seemed.

But no blade fell, and the door opened to reveal Zachary Glass wearing something other than a suit.

"Oh my gosh, you have casual clothes," Bram joked. "This is such a Superman/Clark Kent moment."

Zachary frowned down at his outfit of jeans and a black T-shirt like he'd forgotten what he was wearing.

"You would like Superman," Zachary muttered, but before Bram could explain that he didn't say he *liked* Superman, Zachary asked what he was doing there.

"You're an architect, right? Can you help me draw up some plans for a cat shelter?"

"We already have a cat shelter. It's over on Crow Lane, run by that guy with the long hair who always frowns."

"Rye, yeah. No, I mean small, cat-sized shelters that will go outside. They're for Rye. His idea."

"Oh. Yeah, okay. Come in."

Entering Zachary's house felt like stepping into a museum. Every single thing had a place and there was no clutter anywhere. Every framed piece of art hung perfectly straight, and it was immaculately clean.

"Wow," Bram breathed.

His brother, Thistle, would love this house. Of all of them, it had been hardest for Thistle, growing up in a house of seven people. There was always chaos, always noise. No chance to keep things neat because the second one thing was cleaned up another person was messing up something else. And it wasn't just the clutter of seven people, it was all their parents' DIYs: the kombucha mother, the sourdough starter, the herbs drying for tea and tinctures all over the kitchen, all the indoor plants and the cats, dogs, birds, and occasional goat or chicken that were always wandering in from their smallholding.

Outside you could get a bit of peace and quiet from the humans, but there was always something to be done. The huge garden where most of their produce grew always needed weeding, the goats needed milking, the eggs needed collecting, the beehives needed tending. They were nearly self-sufficient, but it only worked if everyone pitched in.

Bram, on the other hand, had been in his glory. He would tell anyone who asked with absolutely certainty that he'd had the greatest childhood on record. Thistle'd had a great childhood too, but his essential desire for order and peace often ran up against the material and human realities of their family system. He could practically hear Thistle's sigh of relief at this place's order, organization, and peace.

In the middle of what was likely intended to be a dining room was a large adjustable drafting table at standing height. Next to it, a rack held pieces of paper and a wall-mounted shelf sported pencils, pens, rulers, protractors, and other supplies galore. It was like walking into a posh stationery store.

Zachary slid the large sheet of paper that was on the drafting table into one of the waiting cubbies in the rack and replaced it with a fresh piece.

"Okay. What are you thinking?"

The truth was that Bram hadn't thought about the aesthetics of the cat shelters at all, only their function.

"I thought maybe I could tell you what they need and then we could figure out the outside? What they look like doesn't actually matter. The cats won't care."

He smiled, thinking this would make Zachary's job of showing him how to draw a plan easier.

But Zachary's face fell.

"Oh," he said. "Sure. Well, if you just want boxes or whatever..."

"I don't... Well, would you want to come up with some ideas for the design?" Bram asked. He didn't want to make work for Zachary, but the man had seemed so excited for a moment.

"Yeah?" Zachary asked, eyes lighting up again.

"Yes, absolutely." He smiled. "Okay, gimme the specs."

Bram described the necessities that Rye had told him about—the temperature that needed to be maintained, the softness of the bedding—but beyond that, Bram was happy to let Zachary's imagination run wild.

Bram could see in Zachary's face the moment when Zachary began to imagine how the shelters could look.

"Where are they going to?"

"Oh, I'm not sure. Rye mentioned putting some in the woods and some around town."

Zachary nodded. He reached for a pencil—the

sleekest pencil Bram had ever seen: silver and mechanical, it fit perfectly in Zachary's fingers.

His lines were fluid and precise, an image emerging as Bram watched.

It looked like a tree stump on its side, the circular end open and bedding inside.

"Camouflaged so that predators don't find the cats while they're sleeping. But once the cats know it's there they can find it again."

"How would you make the outside?" Bram asked.

Papier-mâché would break down over the winter and any kind of clay or moldable material would take a lot of work to make twenty-some.

Zachary looked at him strangely, like it was obvious.

"I'd use a log."

Bram grinned, then laughed at himself.

"It's really cool. And I think I know someone we can get the logs from. They'll need to be large enough to fit the cats and dry enough to hollow out. Then I could waterproof them."

Zachary nodded absently but he was already sketching again. Something that looked like a bread box, then something that looked kind of like a bookshelf…

Zachary blew out a breath and screwed up the paper.

"What? What were those?"

"They're horribly cheesy."

Bram had a suspicion that what was cheesy to Zachary might just possibly be *cute* by others' standards.

"I'd still like to know."

Zachary sighed heavily and smoothed out the paper.

"Okay, you mentioned Rye wanting some around town. I was thinking about how people hate stray animals because they think they're dirty and disease-ridden. But people *love* cute animal videos because the animals are no threat, and they love shop animals because they seem to belong there. So what if some of the local businesses had the cat shelters near their shops. And they were themed to match. A toolbox one at Matheson's Hardware. A bread box one at Sue's bakery."

His eyes had lit up as he described the idea, even after condemning it for being cheesy, but now he faltered and shrugged.

Bram put his hand on the drawing before Zachary could crumple it again.

"I think that's adorable as hell." Zachary's mouth softened and he blinked, eyes wide. "We could even see if the shops would want to sponsor the boxes—like put a little collection box for bedding and cat food and stuff in the corner of their stores?"

"Sure," Zachary said, shrugging. "I'll leave that part to you and Rye. When he was starting the cat shelter he and the Mathesons got every single person in town to help out somehow." His lip curled.

"Somehow?"

"It helps when everyone likes you, I guess."

The bitterness in his tone surprised Bram. Up to now, he'd only ever seen Zachary completely confident or utterly unconcerned with what anyone else thought.

"Anyway," Zachary said. "You could have the basic shelter shape for all the rectangular shelters and then cut a plywood face for the ones that needed a shape. You can paint right? I assume anyone who can carve a dragon out of a bunch of trees with a chainsaw can wield a paintbrush?"

Bram grinned. "Yeah, I can do it, no problem. So, what other businesses could we do themed ones for?"

"Coffee shop, movie theatre, library, restaurants," Zachary ticked off.

"Oh, for the movie theatre, make it look like velvet curtains with those big tassel things opening on the cats," Bram suggested.

"Cute. A takeout container for a restaurant?"

"Yes! A big to-go cup for the coffee shop."

"Oh, if we did it on its side so there's more room for a cat to curl up, we could make it look like the coffee spilled."

Zachary sketched the cup on its side, so the cat was entering through the top and a spill of coffee was a kind of porch.

"That's amazing! God, I'm so glad I asked you."

Bram grinned at Zachary and for the first time, Zachary beamed back at him. It was a toothy, almost goofy grin of such pure sweetness that Bram felt his heart start to pound.

Zachary looked away first, clearing his throat and looking back at the drawings.

"Uh, a peach for Peach's? Or, um, a peach pie?"

"What's Peach's?"

"Oh, it's a diner. Best pie in town."

"I love pie."

"Well, yeah," Zachary said, as if not liking pie would've indicated a distinct personal failing.

The old Bram—the Before Bram—would've said, *Take me there and let me buy you a piece of pie!*

But the new Bram, the After Bram, shuffled his feet and worried a splinter of wood in his pocket until the moment had evaporated and Zachary was focused on his drawing once more.

Zachary looked focused and intent and happy.

"You like architecture a lot, huh?"

"Well. Yeah. But. Yeah, mostly."

Bram raised an eyebrow.

"Lately things at work have been frustrating. I have all these ideas! All these things I want to make, and the firm I work for...they *hired* me because they said they liked my innovation, but now all they do is tell me to streamline and simplify my designs to cut costs or appeal to a more generic customer."

"Maybe you're working for the wrong firm?" Bram suggested gently.

"Moray and Fisk is the premier firm in the Middle West!" Zachary bristled.

"Okaaay, but what good is prestige if you're not getting to do what you want?"

Zachary narrowed his eyes and Bram prepared to back off.

"Someday they'll see it," Zachary said. "They'll see my vision and they'll give me a shot."

Bram nodded reluctantly. He didn't really think things tended to work that way. In his experience, no one would ever value your vision as much as you did. No one would ever invest in you more than you would. So the best thing you could do was make your own way. But Zachary's eyes burned with a zealous conviction that his talents would be recognized, and it wasn't his place to take that away.

Instead, he asked, "Could I see some of the things you've designed? The un-simplified ones."

"Yeah?" The monomaniacal conviction transmuted instantly into a puppyish excitement that melted Bram's heart. "Okay."

It turned out that Zachary Glass was a freaking genius. Bram didn't see the structures well at first. He wasn't used to translating a plan into an image in his mind. But as Zachary traced the lines of his buildings with a slender finger and painted him a picture in words, Bram could see them.

And they were magnificent.

"How the hell did you think to do it like this?" he asked.

Zachary's face was lit with the fire of passion and now he spoke quickly and animatedly.

"It's all about the interplay of presence and absence in this one." He tapped the paper. "From the upper floors, you look down, and it seems like everything is going on down on the lower floors, because the open space narrows. That makes the people want to leave their rooms and go check out the restaurants and shops down below. Then for the people down below, once they get tired or sick of being around everyone, when they look up, it seems like a haven—more space, more peace. They want to go up to their rooms, and as the elevator rises, they *feel* like they're ascending into the clouds. Did you ever see *The Descent*? No, of course not. It's about this group of friends who go caving together and on one trip, they get stuck in a cave system that's filled with these terrifying—"

Bram became aware, as Zachary cut himself off, that he was clenching the edge of the drafting table, bracing for whatever horrors Zachary was about to spill into his brain.

"Er, these totally cute and friendly fuzzy, uh, bunnies, that they want to escape from because, ya know. Bunnies. So…carrot-hungry."

Bram laughed.

"Anyway, the *point* is that the movie is amazing and harrowing because of the narrowing and widening of the caves and the way you feel as a viewer depending on if the camera is pointed into a narrowing cave or a widening opening. That's where I got the idea for that hotel, I mean. Since you asked," he trailed off.

"I could listen to you talk about this stuff forever," Bram said. It had slipped out before he knew he was going to say it. But it was also true.

Zachary didn't seem to know what to say to that. Then he glanced up at Bram uncertainly. "You said you might want to watch one. Do you?"

Bram wanted to keep hanging out with Zachary more than almost anything, but the idea of watching a horror movie filled him with, well, horror.

"Yeeeessss?"

"Well, so long as you're quite certain and enthusiastic about it."

Bram smiled, but confessed, "I seriously get very freaked out. One time my sisters were watching some sleepaway camp movie with a stabby killer person stabbing everyone." Zachary smiled familiarly. "I accidentally saw some of it while I was going to and from the shower, and I was scared to go out in the dark for weeks."

It had been months, really, and he had only seen maybe five seconds of it, but in that five seconds, a girl with a blond ponytail had been eviscerated. Her life snuffed out in an instant. He shuddered just thinking about it.

"Yeah, I kinda got that," Zachary said. "We could watch a non-scary movie."

The relief that washed through Bram was overwhelming. He was all for overcoming fears, but...er, maybe not just yet. And maybe not this fear.

"Oh. Well then, yeah."

Zachary led him to the couch. Unlike the cozy—that is, beaten-in-by-seven-people—couches of his youth, this one was more art than furniture. It was cool gray with clean lines and a light wooden frame. It also looked like Bram might reduce it to kindling if he flopped down on it.

"Midcentury modern," Zachary said, mistaking Bram's trepidation for curiosity.

Bram lowered himself to the couch very gently. He'd always been large—his whole family was—and when he started working construction his already large frame packed on muscle quickly.

Mostly he liked his body and his stature. It made him feel good, being strong enough to do nearly whatever he wanted to do. But times like this, he wished he could fold himself just a bit smaller.

After thirty seconds of waiting for the couch to creak and threaten, Bram relaxed. It was actually more comfortable than it looked. Which wasn't a mean feat, since it had looked about as comfortable as a graham cracker.

"Okay, what do you want to watch?"

Zachary opened a midcentury highboy hutch—Zachary's words; it was just a cabinet—to reveal a DVD collection.

"I know, I know, who still has DVDs when you can stream everything."

"My parents. Hell, they still have VHS tapes. We never had TV when I was younger, just watched the same videos over and over."

"Could you not afford it?" Zachary asked. His tone was neutral, no judgment or pity, as Bram had often heard when people learned he hadn't gotten new clothes or video games or his own bedroom as a kid.

"Nah, we just lived pretty off the grid. There was a lot of other stuff to do. Take care of the animals, tend the garden, cook. There are a lot of us, so dinner was quite an affair."

Zachary was looking at him with interest.

"Did you live on a commune?" he asked delightedly.

"Not exactly, but my parents would be happy to think so. It was just our family, but there are seven of us, and we grew most of our own food, had goats for milk and cheese, and chickens for eggs."

"Wow. That sounds…"

Zachary paused and seemed to argue with himself about what to say. Some people said it sounded idyllic or perfect or magical. Some said it sounded like hell. All of which were a little bit true.

"Smelly."

Bram laughed. "Yeah, well. Animals do smell like animals."

"Hmm. I don't really know anything about animals."

"Did you grow up in Wyoming?"

A shadow passed over Zachary's face.

"Yes. I grew up in Cheyenne. We moved here when I was sixteen."

That made more sense.

Bram rose and stood behind Zachary to peruse the movies. It was almost all horror, judging by titles like

It Follows, *Repulsion*, and *Drag Me to Hell*. But there were also mysteries and some science fiction, some classic old Hollywood romances.

"Honestly, I don't know what any of these movies are, so I'm not going to be much help."

"What genre are you in the mood for?"

Bram shrugged. "Why don't you just pick something? I'm sure whatever you pick will be great."

"Okay."

Zachary put on a movie called *Let the Right One In*.

"It's not scary," he promised. "Just a little bit spooky. Atmospheric, really."

Bram nodded, and Zachary sank onto the couch beside him.

The movie was about children, but with each swell of ominous strings or camera tracking around a dark corner, Bram felt himself getting more and more tense.

It was a physical reaction—an involuntary cringing back in the face of something that seemed about to hurt him at any moment.

After twenty minutes, Zachary pressed pause.

"Too scary, huh?" he said.

"Huh? No, no. Um. Well. Yeah. Yes. Yep, too scary. God, sorry!"

Zachary laughed. "It's okay. I kind of like that you're so affected by all the musical cues and angles and stuff. I'm so inured to them mostly that I forgot how fun it is to watch with someone who doesn't know the vocabulary."

"I'm just sitting here waiting for something horrible to happen. It's like…like getting dumped. You know something's off even though your partner's acting like everything is fine. Then one day, the hammer falls and you realize why you've felt wrong."

"Oh." Zachary seemed to think about that for a minute. Then he said softly, "I've been dumped but it was always after just a few dates."

"It feels almost cruel," Bram said. "The movie, I mean. Like its goal is to torture you."

Zachary shook his head. "But that's the thing. If you enjoy it, it's not torture, it's…"

"Masochism?" Bram joked.

Zachary frowned.

"I was just kidding. Sorry if I—"

Zachary waved his apology away. "Okay, but listen. The way you feel about horror movies? That's how I feel about exercise. Like, those people who glorify sports training or military training? Running until you vomit? Doing a ropes course in the mud until you're so physically exhausted you collapse. Listening to a coach or a drill sergeant bark orders at you like they're encouraging you to shut off your own brain or awareness of your body and only listen to their commands? That's torture to me. That's masochism. Yet people voluntarily submit to it and our culture glorifies it. I don't want to watch a movie about some teenager training past the point of pain every day to go play a game where he slams other kids' heads into the ground. It's unbearable."

"Never really thought about it like that before."

"Sure, because sports stars are heroes and fascist militarism is lauded in our culture. People who like horror movies are told they're messed up for liking them, whereas people who like football get the message that they're normal."

A dozen other examples came to mind and Bram nodded, realizing Zachary was right.

Zachary stood and ran his fingers along the titles in the cabinet, then plucked out and swapped the disks.

"I think this will be more to your liking."

The Wizard of Oz, the titles announced. Bram relaxed.

"I don't know," he said with a wink. "When that scary witch comes on you might have to hold my hand."

Bram had been kidding. Had been flirting, really. But when the Wicked Witch of the East appeared on the screen, a cool, soft hand slid into his. Zachary kept his eyes on the film, but he squeezed Bram's hand and didn't let go until she'd disappeared in a puff of smoke. Then he turned to Bram with soft eyes.

"You doing okay?"

Bram felt something important liquefy in his gut and swallowed hard.

"I'm doing great."

Zachary kept looking at him and all Bram wanted in that moment was to pull him close and kiss those full lips. "Um," he said instead. "Does this mean our prank war is over?"

Zachary smiled, warm and delighted.

"Not a chance in hell."

Chapter Ten

Zachary

Finally, everything was coming together. Zachary had spent the whole day putting up the first layer of what would be his Halloween decorations, and all was going to plan. It didn't look like much at the moment—the first layer never did—but Zachary saw it all in his head.

The idea had been inspired by his friend Wes' experiments with bioluminescence. It was derived from undersea creatures, and was what gave the depths of the ocean their eerie glow. So Zachary designed a concept that would take place under the sea. He was calling this year's Halloween installation "Ghost Ship." The challenge was in lighting the display so it was visible in the dark, while still maintaining the illusion of an absence of light. But Zachary Glass thrived on a challenge.

And this year, he wasn't just thinking about his display. He was also about thinking of ways to prank Bram.

Bram.

Zachary had spent a *lot* of time thinking about him lately. He'd been surprised when Bram showed up at his house the other day, but it had led to one of the most enjoyable evenings he'd had in some time. Bram had seemed to see what he was doing with his designs and to be genuinely impressed. Zachary smiled remembering his wide blue eyes and his lips parting around "Wow" over and over again.

Zachary grinned. He hoped he'd get an even bigger reaction with the prank he was about to pull.

Gus, Wes' stepdaughter, had really come through for him on this one. Wes had texted him the other day: Gus says a good prank is to set up a table like for dinner and then it's your head. Whatever that means.

But Zachary knew exactly what it meant, and it delighted him.

Which was how he had come to be crouched beneath his own dining table at 7:00 p.m., waiting for Bram to arrive.

He'd invited the other man to dinner and a few minutes ago texted that he should let himself in, as Zachary was occupied cooking.

The knock on the door came, and then it opened.

"Hello? Zachary, I'm here! Don't wanna startle you."

Zachary grinned. Bram was the one who was about to get startled!

The tablecloth hung to the floor all the way around

the table to hide Zachary from view, so he couldn't see Bram, but he could hear his footsteps approach.

"Wow, this looks fancy," Bram called into the kitchen from right in front of the table. "Can I peek?"

Of course Zachary couldn't yell from the kitchen since he was, in fact, under the table, but he was counting on the fact that Bram's curiosity would compel him to lift the silver dome from the platter in the center of the table.

And sure enough…

The silver dome lifted. Zachary's face was fixed in a rictus, and he bit down on the blood capsules. Blood spewed from his mouth and down his chin in a viscous *blerb*.

Zachary had just time enough to see Bram's handsome face horror-struck, before he screamed and the silver dome went flying. It missed the hanging lamp by centimeters and hit the wall with a ringing sound and the crunch of plaster.

Bram clutched his chest. He looked genuinely aghast, and Zachary's stomach fell. Somehow he had let the fact that this idea was thought of by a child convince him it would only be mildly startling, but it was clear that the effect had worked too well for someone as easily scared as Bram.

"I'm so sorry," Zachary said.

More blood poured out of his mouth. It tasted blank and slimy.

Bram winced.

Zachary attempted to extricate himself from underneath the table, but his legs had fallen asleep as he knelt there, and he couldn't quite drag the leaves of the table apart from this angle.

"Er. Any chance you could pull the table leaf out?"

Bram seemed to wake up then, and with one yank, Zachary was free. His head, which had been surrounded by a cardboard platter with a cutout for his neck, popped out, dripping blood, and with a groan, Zachary stood.

"I'm really sorry," he said again, wiping the blood from his mouth with the doily around his neck. "I didn't think this would be scary. I meant it to be funny, but I'm such an asshole and I didn't think how scared you would be. Damn. I'm really sorry."

Bram shook his head.

"I just. Jesus, you really got me."

He pressed his palm flat against his chest as if to check his heart still beat beneath all that muscle.

"I guess I should've known it was a prank when I didn't smell any food, huh? Silly me."

And that was when Zachary noticed that Bram wasn't wearing his usual outfit of worn jeans and a T-shirt (or worn jeans and no shirt at all). He was wearing navy pants and a pale pink short-sleeved button-down shirt that struggled to contain his biceps. He was dressed up. For dinner. With Zachary.

Only there was no dinner.

There was just an empty table covered in blood and Zachary in ratty old clothes he used to paint the walls when he moved in. Also covered in blood.

"Oh," Zachary said softly.

"Er. Yeah. You got me," Bram said. And although he was playing it off with his usual good nature, Zachary thought he could detect a darker emotion beneath that smiley facade.

Zachary wanted to put a hand on his shoulder and apologize again, but both of his hands were sticky with blood. He felt awful and it was very unlike him. He'd won! The prank had worked perfectly—even better than he'd imagined, and he would certainly be telling Gus every detail—but he derived no satisfaction from it. He wanted to replace the stilted smile on Bram's face with his real smile. The broad, unselfconscious one that showed his teeth and crinkled the skin around his eyes.

"Hey, what if we go to Peach's Diner for dinner? My treat?" Zachary offered.

"Oh, you don't have to do that. Good one, ha-ha." Bram said, as if that too were another prank. But he wasn't leaving.

"No, no, I want to. Please." Bram's shoulders relaxed and he put his hands in his pockets. "If you don't mind waiting for me to take a shower and change."

"I'd pretty much insist on it," Bram said. And there was that happy grin.

Peach's Diner was an institution in Garnet Run, and it was one of the few places that Zachary felt at home outside 666 Casper Road.

When his family had moved to Garnet Run at the beginning of his junior year of high school, Zachary hadn't made friends. He hadn't joined clubs or done after-school activities. After all, why would people like him any more here than they had in Cheyenne?

Instead, when he couldn't stand being in his house any longer, when the sound of his mother's voice on the phone, tracking down what she'd believed were leads, had wormed its way into his head such that he absolutely had to get out of the house *now*, he'd taken his sketchbook and his iPod, and he'd come to Peach's Diner.

He'd order a piece of pie and sit at a booth in the back and draw everything that crowded his mind.

Sometimes Melba, who was still a waiter there, would slip him a plate of fries or a grilled cheese sandwich. She'd say a customer had sent it back and it'd just go to waste otherwise, so he didn't need to pay. But even at sixteen, Zachary had seen it for what it was: kindness. An act of kindness for a pitiful boy that no one else was kind to. And he'd loved her for it.

"My favorite customer!" Melba said as they walked in. "Been a long time, sweetie."

"Hey, Melba. How are you?"

"Can't complain, can't complain."

It was her standard answer. Though he had known Melba for twelve years, he knew almost as little about her now as he had the first time he'd come in.

"And who's this?" she asked, with a twinkle.

"Bram Larkspur, ma'am. Nice to meet you."

Melba raised an eyebrow at Zachary, as if to congratulate him on something. Zachary looked at the floor.

When they were seated and had menus, Melba put a hot tea in front of Zachary without asking.

"What's good here?" Bram asked.

"I don't really care about food. You should ask Melba."

Bram goggled.

"You don't…care about it?"

"No. I mean, it's a necessary part of staying alive and all that. I'm just not terribly invested in specific foods as opposed to others."

Bram raised an eyebrow, but just nodded.

"What would you recommend?" he asked Melba. "Just has to be vegetarian."

Melba's eyes got wide at that.

"Well, *not* the veggie burger," she said conspiratorially. "Only a few tourists passing through ever order them, so I think we've had the same box since about 1997."

"Noted. No veggie burger, then."

"You know what," Melba said, sliding the menu from his hand. "I'll just have Cal cook you up something. No meat," she repeated, giving him a thumbs-up.

"Thanks, that'd be great." Bram's smile was irresistible, and Melba smiled right back at him.

"The usual, sweets?"

"Yeah." Zachary handed her his menu.

"What's the usual?" Bram asked.

"Whatever Cal feels like giving me."

When the food came, Zachary's was meatloaf with gravy, mashed potatoes, peas, and a biscuit.

Bram's was a baked sweet potato with cheesy broccoli and sour cream on top, a bowl of chili with corn bread, and a side of mac and cheese.

"Wow," Bram said. "Looks amazing. My thanks to Cal."

Melba winked at him, then mouthed to Zachary, *I love him.*

"Oh my god," Zachary muttered, but Bram didn't seem to notice, too busy tucking into his potato.

Once they'd eaten for a few minutes, Zachary said, "I just want to apologize again for earlier. I should've thought about—"

Bram waved his apology away.

"I get it. You don't have to apologize again. Thanks."

"Okay."

"So does your family live in Garnet Run too?"

Bram asked, firmly changing the subject. Zachary had thought he wanted it changed; but not to this. He nodded.

They lived in the same house as when they'd moved here all those years ago, and which Zachary hadn't returned to in years. When he'd been looking for a place to live himself, the house on Casper Road had appealed to him first because from it he could reach everywhere he might want to go in town without driving past his parents' home.

Bram raised an eyebrow, listening intently.

"It's just my parents. We're not very close."

"Oh," Bram said. "Sorry to hear that. What was it like, being an only child? I can't even imagine. Was it peaceful? I bet it was really peaceful."

Bram was smiling, clearly picturing his own rowdy clan.

"Um, well. I wasn't an only child."

Bram froze.

Zachary didn't talk about this. But then, he didn't talk to people much.

"I have an older sister. Had. Have, I don't know."

Past tense, present tense, so strange for a person to be a tense. To *have* been a tense. No, to be a tense—present, even if the tense is past.

"She disappeared when I was fourteen and she was seventeen. In Cheyenne."

Bram's blue eyes were wells of horror and sympathy.

Zachary looked out the window. It was the same window he'd looked out nearly every day the first year they'd moved here. He'd looked out the window between drawings and he'd wondered if Sarah was looking out a window somewhere too, thinking about him. Thinking at all.

"There was an investigation. Neighbors, Police, FBI. Tracker dogs and helicopters and *Missing* posters."

He'd been tasked with putting those posters on every telephone pole, bulletin board, and bus stop, until his thumb and forefinger blistered from the staple gun and he wondered if his parents would even notice if he didn't come home. His mother was so busy orchestrating her own investigation that after a while even the lead detective on the case seemed to wince when she came near. His father was equally preoccupied with the kind of blank, inner-focused journey that left no evidence for his family, no breadcrumb trail that could be followed, and no indication that contact would be welcome.

"That's…that's a nightmare. Jesus, I'm so sorry. What did they think happened? If you don't mind me asking…"

Zachary hadn't spoken about Sarah in a very long time.

"The police's official conclusion was that she ran away. So after she turned eighteen, about nine months after she disappeared, they stopped looking. They hadn't found any evidence of foul play and they couldn't link Sarah to any criminal behavior."

"Would she have done that? Run away?"

That was the question Zachary had asked himself a thousand times. His mother had dismissed that possibility out of hand—but of course she had. He thought Sarah very well might have left. But she had never been cruel, and it would take real cruelty to put her family through leaving without a trace and never letting them know she was okay.

"I think she left on purpose. But then something happened to her that prevented her from getting in touch."

"But your parents didn't agree?"

"No. My dad gave up when the cops gave up. Not that he didn't care. He just…he's not a creative person. I don't think he had the ability to imagine anything but her dead or wanting nothing to do with us. It made him too sad, so he just stopped talking about it."

"Self-protection," Bram murmured.

It was a generous description.

"And your mom?"

For Zachary, the word *mom* was synonymous with *dogged, obsessive, single-minded, exhausting.* At least it was since Sarah disappeared and his mother decided she had one purpose in life: prove to the world that Sarah had been murdered.

She had believed that she would solve Sarah's case. And for two years she'd spent every moment and dollar trying to do just that.

The local news coverage had dried up and the neighbors had stopped volunteering their Saturdays for search parties, and the cops had said that with no evidence they couldn't devote further resources to the case.

It had made sense to Zachary. Sarah was just one person. She couldn't be the focus of everyone's energy forever. No one could.

But his mother took the public falling off as a personal betrayal. A grand injustice that signified everything that was wrong with the world, and nothing could convince her otherwise.

"My mother loves the case more than she ever loved having Sarah in her life."

He bit his lip. He hadn't meant to say that out loud. He wasn't even entirely sure it was true. His mother loved Sarah, but they hadn't had an easy relationship. Without Sarah there, his mother had been able to re-imagine their relationship exactly as she pleased.

Bram didn't try to soothe him. No *I'm sure that's not true* bullshit. Bram just said, "What about you?"

"What about me what?"

"Does she love her relationship with Sarah's case more than she loves you?"

"Yeah."

And that was the truth.

Bram's eyes welled with empathy.

"That must be pretty hard?"

Zachary shrugged.

It had. He was there and Sarah was gone. To his mother that meant Zachary was fine and Sarah needed her. But the truth was that Zachary had *not* been fine. He *had* needed her. And Sarah was probably dead. So. Bad choice, Mom.

"She just…she wants to talk about it all the time. Still. She asks me to help her put out information on-line. She has a subreddit. She's…"

"Fixated."

It was the right word.

"It's the defining thing in her life. She's *Sarah Glass' mother.* There just isn't much room for anyone else in her life because no one else knows what it's like to be Sarah Glass' mother. She, conveniently, is always going to be the expert."

"What about your dad?"

"Oh, he's not Sarah Glass' mother either, so he doesn't count."

Bram nodded.

"Is he Zachary Glass' father?"

"Sometimes. He likes quantitative successes. It's easy to know what to say to them."

Bram opened his mouth and then closed it.

"I can't even imagine," he said. "In some ways, I think if one of my siblings disappeared, maybe I'd be like your mom."

Zachary knew what he meant. Bram meant that he loved them so much he'd never give up on them. But that wasn't the way it worked. And that wouldn't make him similar to Zachary's mom, because that wasn't how she felt.

"I don't think you would. Because you know they wouldn't want your life to become about them and only them. You know they wouldn't want you to stop living just because they might've."

Bram froze with his fork halfway to his mouth.

"You're right."

Zachary nodded. If there was one thing he felt confident about it was his ability to determine who would and would not become monomaniacally fixated on the cold case of someone they loved.

Too bad there wasn't much call for that.

"My dad wanted to move. After Sarah. He didn't want to be in the house where she'd disappeared from. It was too hard for him. My mom refused because what if Sarah came back and we weren't there."

Bram winced.

"They fought about it for a year. Then my dad lived

in a hotel for six months until he could convince her to move."

"And you came to Garnet Run. Do you have family here or something?"

Zachary huffed out a dark laugh.

"Nope. My mom thought Sarah might have come here at some point. A psychic told her so."

Bram nodded as if psychics were a commonplace source of information, so Zachary went on.

"She'd consulted a few but she became friendly—kind of—with one. I'm not sure what she said the connection was. I know my mom told us, but it's been a long time."

After the fact. She'd told them after the fact—months after, in fact. Once their Cheyenne house had been sold and Zachary had started school at Garnet Run High.

He woke early one morning. Hours before school. To them arguing in bitten-back voices in the kitchen.

"That's how we ended up in this nowhere town? A goddamn psychic? This is still about Sarah and all I wanted was the chance to be a family again."

"We'll *be* a family again when Sarah comes home!" his mother had snarled.

Zachary had pulled the blanket over his head and wondered if he'd ever not be haunted by the sister who was more a part of his life now that she was gone than she'd been when she was there.

But Garnet Run had turned out to be good for Zachary. The students at his new school knew him as the new kid, and there were few enough new arrivals to Garnet Run that this made him an object of curiosity rather than approbation. They were interested in him coming from "the city." Interested enough, anyway, that he was able to make a few casual friends and not dread going to school so much that he was consumed by constant dread.

It helped that no one here knew about Sarah. And he certainly wasn't going to tell them.

That had been one of the strangest things: the first day after Sarah's disappearance at his old school, the people who had tormented him didn't know what to do. Nothing about *him* had changed. All their insults were still relevant. But as they opened their mouths to sling them, they remembered that something tragic had just happened to him and they didn't say them. It was as if some higher, greater power than they had bullied Zachary, so they didn't feel they had to.

It had worn off, of course.

So, yeah, Zachary didn't care how they'd ended up here; he'd just been glad to leave Cheyenne.

"Sorry," Zachary said into the awkward silence. "I know this whole conversation is kind of a downer."

Bram shook his head. "It's your past."

And that, of course, was undeniable.

Chapter Eleven

Bram

Can I make dinner up to you? the text from Zachary had said. They're showing The Wolf Man at the Odeon on Saturday. It's a total classic (and not too scary, I swear). What do you say?

Bram had smiled at "and not too scary."

I'm in, he'd replied.

The idea of Saturday Nights at the Odeon seemed to be recapturing the glamour of a bygone era of moviegoing. Or so the website suggested, with patrons encouraged to dress up and leave their phones at home.

Bram knocked on Zachary's door at precisely 7:20 p.m. Zachary had been very specific. Bram grinned. He was strangely charmed by the other man's attention to detail. Time had been a flexible and relative thing in his house growing up. It'd kind of had to be, with so many people jockeying for cereal and showers and the spot closest to the fire. Life with animals and gardens was about rhythm and sun and rain, not numbers on a clock. Left to his own devices, that was still how Bram preferred it—rising with the sun and letting the elements shape his day.

Zachary opened the door and Bram's eyes got wide.

He always wore a suit on weekdays, and that was what Bram had assumed he'd wear tonight. In fact, he'd dressed to match. But Zachary was wearing wool trousers, a long-sleeved button-down, and a tight-fitting vest that exaggerated his slim build.

His curly dark hair was parted on the side and slicked back unsuccessfully, but Bram rejoiced at its resistance.

He looked amazing.

"You look amazing," Bram said.

Zachary was blinking up at him appreciatively and it kindled an answering fire in Bram's stomach.

"Oh, um. Thanks. You always look…yeah."

Zachary shoved a hand through his hair, then rolled his eyes at himself for messing it up.

"Do you want to take my bike?" Bram asked, then, at Zachary's confusion, clarified, "My motorcycle? I have an extra helmet."

Zachary looked suspicious. "I've never ridden a motorcycle."

"You don't have to do anything but hold on."

With a ginger pat to his hair, Zachary shrugged. "Okay. Just please don't kill me."

"I will do my best."

"Or, like, scrape me across the pavement until half my body is sanded off."

"Gah, Jesus, ugh." Bram shuddered at the image.

"Oops, sorry."

"I really hope that comment isn't indicative of your estimation of how scary this movie is."

"It's really not, I swear. There will be children there."

That didn't do much to comfort Bram. Moon and Thistle had loved gory, terrifying comics as kids and Bram had hidden them under the bed because the covers gave him nightmares.

He handed Zachary his spare helmet and straddled the bike, holding out a hand to Zachary for balance.

Zachary settled lightly on the bike and Bram showed him where to put his feet. He smiled at Zachary's bright red dress socks.

"Put your arms around my waist and let your center of gravity shift along with mine. Don't worry if it feels like the bike leans a bit going around curves. That's normal and it doesn't mean we're falling over. Okay?"

Zachary muttered something but muffled it in Bram's shoulder. He slid his arms around Bram's waist and blew out a hair-ruffling breath.

"Okay," he said.

A string of curses trailed behind them as the bike revved and began to move, then all Bram could attend to besides the road was the warm press of Zachary Glass against his back.

Zachary's arms were tight around his waist, but after a few blocks, he relaxed and flattened his palms against Bram's stomach. Bram was sure he could feel every finger where it pressed against him.

As they hit the long stretch of straight road between their neighborhood and Main Street, and the bike picked up speed, Zachary let out a whoop of joy that made Bram light with happiness. He loved the feel of wind against his face, rushing through a landscape unmediated by glass or metal. He could feel Zachary looking around, could feel the intimate press of his chin against his shoulder.

They arrived at the Odeon far too soon for Bram.

"What's the verdict?" he asked Zachary, dismounting and turning to help him off the bike.

Zachary's hand was warm from Bram's stomach and when he took off his helmet, his hair was back to its usual riot of glorious curls.

"That," Zachary said, eyes wild and tearing from the ride, "was absolutely stupendous."

Joy rushed through Bram as he imagined all the rides he'd love to take Zachary on now that he liked the bike.

They grinned at each other like excited kids as they walked into the theater.

The Odeon was stunning. Inside, it looked like an old-fashioned theater out of a glamorous Hollywood movie. The ticket booth and refreshments areas were elaborate and gilt, the ceiling housed an enormous crystal chandelier that spangled moviegoers with light, and the geometric patterned carpet was luxe.

"Wow."

Zachary agreed. "This style of glam deco design is rarely restored well, so it's a treat to see it respected."

He went on to point out the hallmarks of the design style, but Bram found himself distracted by the man himself. Zachary's face transformed when he spoke about architecture and design. His usually stern brows raised and softened, and he gestured fluidly.

As he was in the middle of saying something about

geometry and light, a little girl ran up and threw her arms around him.

"Oof. Oh, hey, Gus."

"Mr. Glass," she said. "I know your secret."

"Uh. You do?"

Two men caught up to the little girl. One was tall and broad and had shaved brown hair and a watchful expression. The other was small and blond, and it took Bram a moment to place him as the man he'd met in Matheson's hardware store and the daughter he absolutely, positively could not inform about chainsaw sculpture.

"Hey!" the blond man—Adam, right—said. "You guys know each other?"

"*You* guys know each other?" Bram asked, as Zachary said, "We're neighbors."

The tall brunet said nothing, but Bram got the sense he was paying close attention.

"Wes, this is Bram, short for Bramble," Zachary said with uncharacteristic casualness and a pointed look that was probably intended to be subtle but made Bram almost certain that Zachary had already told this man about him.

"Hi, I'm Wes," he said and held out a hand.

They shook, and Bram nodded.

"Daddy, can I *please* have fancy popcorn?" Gus asked.

"Yes, you can have fancy popcorn," Adam said, and then immediately ran after his daughter, who sprinted to the concession stand.

"What's fancy about the popcorn?" Bram asked the group, stomach rumbling.

"It doesn't come from a microwave," Wes said. His voice was low and tinged with humor.

For some reason, Bram had thought of Zachary as a solitary soul, but he seemed to know a lot of the people attending the screening. He'd been introduced to Cameron, Henry's partner, someone named Marie, whom he'd seen at Matheson's Hardware but never spoken to, and a smattering of others.

"It's a small town," was all Zachary said when Bram mentioned it.

They sat with Adam, Wes, and Gus. Used to his nieces and nephews who preferred running around outside to sitting down, Bram was surprised that the moment the lights dimmed, Gus was fixated on the screen.

Henry, dressed to the nines, red hair slicked into a pompadour, tapped the microphone.

"Welcome to *Thirty Nights of Spooky Cinema* at the Odeon! Thank you all for being here. This kicks off our Halloween Horror month. *The Wolf Man* is a classic of horror cinema and one of the Universal Monsters movies that so deeply influenced the depictions of horror characters moving forward. Lon Chaney Junior's wolf makeup took five or six hours to apply and a full hour to remove. The Wolf Man is the only one of the Universal Monsters to be played by the same actor in all film versions. I hope you enjoy it. And beware the bright light of an autumn moon," he finished spookily.

Zachary had been right. The movie wasn't too scary. In fact, there was something mournful about the character of the Wolf Man. Bram looked over to see Zachary utterly absorbed.

When Zachary noticed him looking, he whispered, "Did you get scared?"

No judgment. No disapproval. Just concern. Bram wanted to say yes, because he wondered what Zachary would do. He waited a beat too long to respond and Zachary held out his hand tentatively.

Bram's heart pounded as he slid his hand into Zachary's. Their gazes held for a moment, and Zachary gave a small smile, then turned back to the screen.

At the end, when the werewolf died, Bram thought he saw a tear at the inner corner of one of Zachary's dark eyes.

As the lights came up, Gus, who'd ended up on Wes' lap halfway through the movie, lifted her head up, snarled, and let out a wild howl.

Heads turned toward them, and Wes ducked his head behind Gus, like he wanted to hide. But from around the theater came answering howls as the town of Garnet Run welcomed Halloween.

Goodbyes said, they stepped into the cool night air and Bram grinned. For the first time since leaving Olympia, he'd felt like a part of something. Even if that something was—of all things—a horror movie.

He hadn't realized how much he'd missed it, that sense of belonging, of being part of something larger than himself. Of not being alone.

He tipped his head back to the night sky and howled.

Zachary snorted and kept walking. Bram jogged after him, put his hands on his shoulders, and squeezed, howling again.

"You're ridiculous," Zachary said, voice very proper. Then he turned, looked up, and pointed at the sky with a trembling finger. "Oh god," he said, voice shaking. "It's...the light of an autumn moon. It's...changing me."

Then he lifted his own delicately pointed chin to the sky and howled.

From behind them, moviegoers streaming out of the Odeon took up the howl, until Main Street echoed with cries to the moon.

They were laughing and falling over each other when they reached the motorcycle.

Zachary's face was lit with happiness and mischief (not to mention the light of the autumn moon). His curls were in total disarray and he had a smear of chocolate in the corner of his mouth.

He was beautiful. How had Bram never noticed?

He reached out and gently wiped the chocolate away with his thumb.

"You just had some..."

Zachary's eyes widened as Bram brushed his skin, and his lips parted. When Bram's hand dropped to his side, Zachary's tongue appeared for a moment, as if he wanted to taste the place Bram had touched.

Then he looked away and jammed the helmet on.

"Okay, ready?" Bram asked as he revved the bike.

Zachary squeezed his shoulders, then snaked his arms around his waist. He rested his chin on Bram's back, and Bram's heart went all funny.

The first time Bram rode a motorcycle he'd been sixteen and had a crush on Nathan Adamson, who'd graduated the year before. When Nathan took him for a ride, he'd fallen in love. His affair with Nathan only lasted about a week—long enough for him to realize that attractiveness is no guarantee of character—but his love affair with motorcycles had never waned.

He drove toward home, but instead of turning onto Casper Road, he took the road up into the pine forest north of town. He felt Zachary tense against him for a moment, then relax.

Away from traffic lights, Bram opened the bike up, zooming smoothly through the moonlit night.

Somewhere ahead of them, a hawk dove—black form peeling itself elegantly from the darkness—and Bram felt akin to it, the bike the closest he'd ever get to flying.

They reached a crest in the road and the moon came into view. Bram slowed and let the bike come to a stop.

They stood and looked at the moon in silence.

"Imagine if you could just take off," Zachary said softly. "Soar like that hawk over the land."

It was so close to what Bram had been thinking a minute before it felt like Zachary had plucked the thought from his head.

Bram nodded.

"It seems peaceful," he said. "And exhilarating."

"Yeah. Lonely, though," Zachary said.

They stood side by side, arms pressing together, a warm spot in the cool night.

Bram turned at the same moment Zachary did. They blinked at each other, and in Zachary's eyes, Bram saw desire and uncertainty in equal measure.

Zachary blinked and the spell was broken. Bram cleared his throat and got back on the bike.

When they turned onto Casper Road, Bram wished they were back up in the clouds, in the dark, with the moon.

Zachary handed him the helmet and smiled a bit awkwardly.

"Thanks for coming with me," he said. "It was fun."

"It was," Bram said. "Thanks for making sure I didn't get too scared."

He was stalling. He knew he was stalling. They were standing in the middle of the street, equidistant from both their houses and stalling. But Bram couldn't quite say anything else.

"You're welcome," Zachary said. "Well. Good night."

"Night," Bram echoed, and went inside by the light of the autumn moon.

Chapter Twelve

Zachary

There was no doubt about it. This was going to be the prank that won the prank war.

As long as Zachary didn't fall to his death first.

He tested the branch beneath his foot, then inched out onto it, banner rolled up and stuffed underneath his sweater.

He could already imagine Bram's shock when he went outside the next morning to work on his decorations and found that his own house was an advertisement for Zachary's victory.

Victory. What a delicious word.

The wind picked up and Zachary grabbed for an overhead branch to steady himself.

He inched forward, eyes on the shutters of the right-most window, which would make a good anchor for this side of the banner.

He eased the twine from his back pocket and braced himself on the branch. Now that he was up here, he could see that he wouldn't be able to get as close as he'd hoped. But if he went down one branch…

Zachary eased himself to sitting on the branch, toes reaching for the one below. When he found it, he shuffled down.

Holding on to one branch—nearly hanging from it—as he slid to the other, he had a moment of terrifying vertigo when he thought he'd slipped.

But it wasn't him that was moving. It was the window.

It was sliding open.

Zachary froze.

Bram's face appeared and Zachary could see that the window he'd been about to affix the banner to was in Bram's bedroom. The other man was wearing sweatpants and no shirt and even though Zachary had seen him shirtless before while he worked on his chainsaw carvings, in this context, he was…

Zachary gripped the branch even harder and forced himself to concentrate on not dying.

"Um. Hello there," he said making his voice as casual as possible and sliding the twine back into his pocket. "Lovely night we're having, hmm?"

Bram's smile managed to be amused and wolfish at the same time.

"You know," Bram said, voice gravelly with sleep. "If you wanted to be invited into my bedroom, there were easier ways to go about it."

A wave of lust hit Zachary.

"That right?"

Bram nodded and held out his hand.

It was not the most graceful start to a sexual encounter Zachary had ever had, but honestly? It wasn't the clumsiest either.

Bram grabbed his hand and helped him to the windowsill. As Zachary was hauled inside, the banner slid partway from under his sweater and snagged on the tree branch. Breathing hard, Zachary pushed himself the final bit of the way inside, arms and legs shaking from the effort.

Bram peered out the window.

"Did you climb the tree?"

"Uh-huh."

"Well, that's a security hazard," Bram muttered. But he looked impressed. "Let's see it, then."

"Hmm?"

Bram gestured to the banner that was half rolled under Zachary's sweater and half trailing behind him out the window in tatters.

Suddenly faced with unrolling his banner, Zachary got self-conscious.

"It's silly. Never mind," he said.

Bram smiled softly, seeming to accept that answer.

The moonlight painted Bram's muscular torso silver, highlighting each dip and bulge. Chainsaw carving really was a workout, apparently.

Prank forgotten, Zachary took a step closer and let himself reach out a hand and press his palm to Bram's thick chest. He had springy light brown chest hair and beneath it his skin felt warm even in the cool night air.

"Zachary," Bram murmured.

He caught Zachary's hand and hugged it to him.

Zachary was overwhelmed by his affection for the

big man. There was something so endearing about him. His openness and his humor. His strength and his cheer.

"I wanted to kiss you on Saturday," Bram said, blue eyes dark and intent.

Zachary nodded, words having apparently fled.

"Under the moon," Bram murmured.

Zachary was struck with the urge to howl in response and had rarely been gladder of anything than that he managed to hold it in.

Bram made him feel wild, untethered, outside the rules.

It was dangerous and intoxicating. Unfamiliar. And a little bit scary.

He could feel the heat Bram was giving off, sense the promise of strength in those muscular arms.

Bram murmured his name again. This time it was a question.

Zachary closed the distance between them and took Bram's shoulders in his hands.

"Too damn tall," he muttered, then stood on his tiptoes and pressed his lips to Bram's.

Immediately, Bram's arms came around him and he was gathered in to his warm chest.

Bram's lips were soft, and he kissed with such enthusiasm, as if he were savoring every single sensation.

They stumbled backward, lost in one another, and ended up on the bed, Zachary on top of Bram.

He paused for a moment worrying that he'd squashed Bram, but Bram just smiled a bit shyly and said, "Hey."

Zachary laughed.

"Hey."

He dropped a playful kiss on Bram's chin, but loved

the feel and scent of his skin so much that he trailed kisses along his jaw to his neck.

When he kissed Bram's neck, Bram sucked in a breath and tangled his fingers in Zachary's hair.

Then Bram's mouth was back on his and they were kissing passionately, tongues sliding together in a velvet caress.

They kissed until Zachary's skin felt tight and hot and his lips tingled.

When they finally broke apart, he pressed his forehead to Bram's and they stared at each other, breathing heavily.

"Wow," Bram murmured.

Zachary couldn't agree more.

He moved back in for another kiss, but Bram pulled him close and smothered him in a full body snuggle.

Zachary moaned. He was so turned on he felt swollen and hypersensitive, but it was so good to have Bram's arms around him.

He pressed his hips forward and found an answering hardness.

Bram's breath caught at the contact and he buried his face in the crook of Zachary's neck.

"Do you want…?" Bram murmured.

Zachary nodded and threw his leg over Bram's hip.

They ground together slowly and hot pleasure tore through Zachary until he shuddered.

Bram made a muffled sound and then they were locked together, entwined as they thrust and moaned.

Zachary's whole body turned into a humming, electric buzz and he strained toward the promise of exquisite explosion.

Bram held him close, muscles taut and straining.

"Oh, god," Bram moaned, and then he threw his head back and clutched Zachary to him as he came.

The heat and strength of Bram's body were electric, and Zachary felt his orgasm start to build. Bram reached down and cupped his erection, and his touch was exquisite, even through fabric.

Zachary strained and Bram stroked him until the spark caught and ecstasy roared through Zachary, growing as it spread like ripples in a stream.

With one final wave of heat, Zachary collapsed into Bram's arms, panting and shuddering, tiny aftershocks sending frissons through his electrified skin.

He moaned and let himself go completely boneless against Bram.

Bram gathered him close and hugged him like a teddy bear. Only, you know, hot.

Their lips found each other and this time the kisses were familiar, sweet, appreciative.

Chapter Thirteen

Bram

Zachary Glass was hot as hell. Uninhibited and gorgeous and sensual, and Bram didn't want to let him go.

Bram had watched him teeter on the tree outside his bedroom window, clearly perpetrating some absurd prank. Though Bram had kind of assumed they were done with the prank war since they'd started spending real time together, somehow he was amused that Zachary saw no reason to stop. He'd felt a moment of utter gutting fear when Zachary's foot had slipped and he would've fallen if he hadn't caught himself.

Now, safe in his arms, satisfied and spent, Zachary's hot cheek was pressed against Bram's shoulder, and despite an uncomfortable mess in his pants, Bram couldn't even think about untangling from him.

"You're amazing," Bram murmured into his hair.

That got a suspicious snort followed by a nuzzle that spoke volumes.

They lay there for a while, drifting in and out of sleep, until Zachary pulled away and made a face at his own crotch.

"Um."

"You can borrow some sweats," Bram offered.

"Okay. Thanks."

And Bram's heart leapt, because maybe that meant he'd stay.

They got cleaned up, soothed a curious Hemlock back to sleep, and then climbed back into bed.

Zachary fit perfectly in his arms and they settled down, sighing.

Bram kissed Zachary's tousled curls.

He wanted to ask Zachary about everything he liked in bed, everything he liked, *period*.

He heard his father's sympathetic sigh when Bram told him about Naveen and Drake.

"Oh, son," he'd said. "You love so big and so true. It's beautiful but it'll break your heart."

And it had.

Bram knew he fell hard for people…but what other way was there to fall?

He slid his hand under Zachary's sweater and stroked the warm skin of his back, tracing the landscape of his spine.

"Do you, um, do this often?" Zachary asked, pushing up on one elbow to look into Bram's face.

"No."

"Oh. Okay."

"I broke up with someone a few months before I

moved here. We were together for a long time. Haven't been with anyone since."

Zachary sat up and raised his eyebrows in question.

"I wondered how you ended up here," he said.

Bram nodded.

"My family used to come to Wyoming to camp when I was a kid. Near Medicine Bow-Routt National Forest. I always loved it. It was so peaceful here, so beautiful. It was the place I had the fondest memories of—besides home, and I couldn't be at home."

"Bad breakup?"

"Yeah."

"What happened?"

Bram liked how Zachary just asked when he wanted to know things.

"I was with Drake for two years. Naveen was my best friend. He was like another brother. My whole family knows him."

Zachary's face was set in an I-think-I-know-where-this-is-going-and-I-hate-it expression.

"Yeah. They cheated on me. *Were* cheating on me for months, it turned out."

He'd walked in on them when he dropped by Naveen's house to borrow a tool. He had been utterly stunned.

Drake, Naveen, and Bram spent a lot of time together and Bram had never noticed anything between them. He'd felt like the luckiest guy alive, that they got along so well, because it meant he got to hang out with his best friend and his boyfriend at the same time.

The truth was that if Drake had told him he had feelings for Naveen, Bram probably would have given his blessing. They had agreed to monogamy, but there was always room for renegotiation. Flexibility was what let people grow and thrive.

But Naveen and Drake had snuck around behind his back instead. When he opened the door, they'd stopped in what would have been a comical frieze, if that frieze hadn't broken Bram's heart.

"To be honest, losing Naveen was worse. We'd been friends since we were ten. I'd told him how much I loved Drake. He knew how much it would hurt me and did it anyway."

"Damn," Zachary said. "That's so heartless."

"I think... I think maybe they fell in love."

This was a new thought that had crept slowly into Bram's mind over the last few weeks. His shock and hurt were so huge and so sharp that for a while they were all he could see. Betrayal, cruelty. He didn't look for explanations because none of them would matter. But now... Naveen wasn't cruel, and he didn't hurt people if he could help it. It was possible he simply...felt things.

"Does that make it better?" Zachary asked doubt-fully.

"Yeah." Bram traced the lines of Zachary's face. "It does."

Zachary shrugged like he didn't agree but his eyes fell shut at Bram's touch.

"You left your family and came to a place where you don't know anyone. It must have been bad."

It really was.

"I got all messed up. I was devastated about Naveen and Drake, but... I couldn't see past the realization that maybe trust is never possible. I guess maybe it sounds naive, but I trusted people. I believed them when they said things. Of course I knew people lied, but a lie or two doesn't mean you can't trust someone when it counts.

"But in the months after, I lost it. That feeling that people—that the world—can be counted on for anything. I started thinking how fragile it all was. That everything we think and believe is based on assuming you can trust people to do what they say or remain consistent in their feelings. And if we can't, then… there's nothing certain. Nothing you can believe in. It messed me up."

Zachary *hmm*ed.

"I don't think I've ever trusted anyone the way you're describing. It's always seemed to me like people are going to do whatever serves their interest and I usually won't know why they're doing it. But that means I have to take care of myself because no one else is going to do it."

Bram ached at the idea.

"My sister Moon says the way I used to think was just privilege plus stupidity, so maybe you're right."

Zachary snorted. "I don't like lies," he said. "If you can't even trust people to do what they say, I want them to at least not make it more complicated."

They lay in silence for a while and Bram stroked Zachary's curls. But just as he was starting to drift off, Zachary said, "You wouldn't know."

"Hmm?"

"Your boyfriend and your friend. Even if there were signs." Bram tensed but Zachary went on. "Knowing would've meant being suspicious. Assuming the worst of them. And you're too generous for that."

Bram buried his face in Zachary's neck.

That was pretty much what his parents had said. But from them, *generous* had felt synonymous with *clueless* or *naive*. When Zachary said it, though—pragmatic, prickly Zachary—it simply felt like *generous*.

"That a compliment?" Bram ventured.

"Not really. Just a statement of fact."

And that was the biggest compliment.

"I guess I don't want to be suspicious," he told Zachary.

"'Course you don't," Zachary said on a yawn. "You'd rather expect the best of someone and be disappointed. You can handle it."

Zachary's breathing deepened as he drifted off to sleep, but Bram lay awake for a long time.

You can handle it.

He'd never thought about it that way, but Zachary had seen to the heart of him. He *could* handle the disappointment of being wrong about someone. He didn't like it. Didn't welcome it. But he could take it.

What he could not handle? Was moving through the world only having relationships based on suspicion and mistrust. That would fundamentally change who he was as a person.

When he'd first met Zachary, he'd found him a bit prickly and off-putting. But apparently he'd been seeing Bram quite clearly. It was humbling and flattering in equal measure.

Bram smiled and closed his eyes. He pulled Zachary even closer and wrapped them up together, luxuriating in the warm press of flesh and hair and the tickle of Zachary's breath against his neck.

Chapter Fourteen

Zachary

"The position is in Denver, and would involve more responsibility and oversight with regard to others' projects," Zachary's boss concluded. "Are you interested?"

"Yes," Zachary said immediately. "Yes, thank you."

They discussed the details and Zachary wrote them down, but all he could think was, *This is what I've been working toward. Recognition from the bosses, finally.*

"Yes sir, thank you for the opportunity I'll see you on Friday."

It was the brass ring and Zachary had been chasing it for his tenure at Moray and Fisk. He'd be the youngest junior partner in the company if he got the promotion.

Here it was: every time they'd told him his designs

were too complicated, too expensive, too odd, *this* was what they were preparing him for—being able to make decisions that would benefit the company, having a big-picture sense of all elements of the project.

Zachary looked in the mirror and spoke to himself. "This is what success looks like. This is what you've been working toward. Do *not* mess it up."

Decorations were starting to appear up and down Casper Road.

Bram and Zachary looped around the cul-de-sac, Hemlock sniffing the air was they went. Zachary took stock of the competition and sniffed as well.

Nonexistent.

Bram pointed at a die-cut ghost sitting on Mrs. Montmorency's porch and grinned, delighted. He was delighted by snowfall, though, so.

No, there was no competition here. Except Bram. But Zachary didn't really think of Bram as competition anymore. In fact, he was having more fun with their prank war than he was with his own decorations. And he'd never thought anything could be more fun than that.

Well, maybe one thing. Zachary shivered as he remembered the exquisite pleasure of Bram's body against his. He supposed maybe you weren't supposed to keep pranking someone once you were sleeping with them… He would text Wes and ask his opinion. Wes was always good for that kind of thing.

The Purcells, the family who owned the house just past the bend in Casper Road, had decorated their entire yard in orange fairy lights. Well, they were supposed to be black and orange, but since black lights just looked like non-lights, it was a sea of orange lights.

Despite this extremely underwhelming effect, Mr. Purcell looked proud. He gestured at the lights around him as they walked past and grinned, as if to say, *Great, right?! Go, Casper Road!*

Zachary set his face in neutral to stop himself sneering, but Bram smiled widely and gave Mr. Purcell the thumbs-up.

"Looks great!" he called.

Mr. Purcell beamed.

Zachary questioned how he and Bram were… whatever they were. He bit his lip, about to ask Bram what they actually were. But the moment they were out of earshot, Bram pulled him close and said, conspiratorially, "Okay, I have an idea."

They crept around in the dark, giggling like schoolboys. Well, like Zachary imagined schoolboys giggled, anyway. He'd always been mostly alone so he supposed he really didn't know.

Solitude was a habit and Zachary had been living it for a long time. But like so many habits, it was one born more of circumstance than choice. And in the weeks since he and Bram had begun spending time together, Zachary's sense of it as a default had melted away.

Before, there had been only a Zachary, so life was one way. Now, there was also a Bram, and so life was another way. Now, in the mornings, part of his routine was setting two alarms—the one that woke him as usual, and the one that made him stop kissing Bram (who had turned out to be a major morning snuggler) and get out of bed.

Now, there was someone else to take into account

when deciding what movie to watch or what to have for dinner.

And somehow it didn't feel like he was losing anything when they watched the documentaries that made Bram lean in close, eyes wide with fascination, the light comedies that made Bram smile softly, or the dramas that made him wipe at his eyes and say, "Aw, man, that one really got me."

Or by eating roasted vegetables and couscous and something called jackfruit, about which Bram always said, "it's perfect for barbecue—no one would know it wasn't pork." Zachary nodded because he was fairly certain that he wouldn't know pork from any other meat anyway, much less a fruit.

Zachary didn't feel like he was losing anything because, of course, he could just watch the movies he wanted and eat the foods he usually ate once Bram was gone and he had to return to his solitary life.

For now, though, it was nice to have someone to share things with.

More than nice. Disturbingly great. So great that actually Zachary was concerned it wouldn't be quite so easy as he'd thought to go back to that pre-Bram life whenever Bram inevitably left him.

Zachary had dated other people. He'd done online dating and he'd been set up by several well-meaning Garnet Run citizens over the years. He'd met the odd person at the grocery store or in a coffee shop.

But although some of them were interesting or attractive or whatever had drawn Zachary to them in the first place, what they *weren't* was worth interrupting his routines for.

He didn't come right out and say this, of course. But

apparently he communicated it to them clearly enough that they took their leave after three or four dates.

And Zachary was fine with it.

But Bram…

This one was really going to hurt.

"C'mere, c'mere," Bram said, dragging him into the shadows. "You hold this end and I'll unroll them."

Zachary nodded and crouched low. It would be great not to have the cops called because someone spotted them creeping around in the yard.

Bram, for all that he was a large man, moved lightly, and his height came in handy, since they couldn't very well be moving a ladder around the Purcells' yard without being noticed.

Bram grinned every time their eyes met, and Zachary found himself grinning right back.

When the final light was in place, they fell against each other, wheezing with the attempt to stay silent.

Bram shook with laughter and wiped at his eyes.

"Aw, man," he said, and buried his face in Zachary's shoulder to muffle his giggles.

"It's a little anticlimactic since we have to wait until tomorrow for them to turn them on," Zachary said, but he said it lightly because he was stroking Bram's hair and it was hard to be disappointed by anything when he was stroking Bram's hair.

"I've done recon," Bram said. "They turn the lights on at 3:30. So we can just casually walk Hem and see it all happen."

"You can. I'll be at work."

"Right, but, you work from home ten houses down. Can't you take a break for like fifteen minutes to watch the fruits of our labor?"

"I don't take a break at 3:30," Zachary said.

Bram's smile faded and it seemed like he wanted to say something else, but he just nodded.

"Okay," he said. "Your call."

He ran a hand through his hair and Zachary was instantly disappointed it wasn't his hand.

There was no concrete reason he couldn't take a break the next day at 3:30. Just because he didn't usually didn't mean he couldn't. No one would know. And this *was* the first time they were joining forces to prank someone else—it seemed like a new phase of the prank war, and Zachary did want to see it. He wouldn't mind seeing the joy on Bram's face either...

"Okay," he said. "I'll meet you outside at 3:25."

Bram's face lit up. "Actually, 3:26 is better for me, schedule-wise," he teased.

Zachary elbowed him and walked away.

He couldn't stop smiling.

Chapter Fifteen

Bram

Bram was standing outside Zachary's front door at precisely 3:25. He didn't want to give Zachary a single moment to regret taking a break from the schedule that was so important to him.

"Hey, handsome," he said when Zachary emerged. Zachary's eyes widened and he opened his mouth and closed it again.

"Hi."

Bram enjoyed flustering Zachary. He was clearly unused to people finding him attractive and Bram took advantage of it to watch him blink and sputter and, eventually, get a tiny private smile at the corners of his mouth, like he was eating something delicious very slowly, so he'd have a little bit to savor later.

"Can a coconspirator get a kiss?" Bram asked.

Zachary's kisses were wild and intense when they were in bed together—hot as hell and unexpected—but there was something deeply tender about the soft kiss Zachary pressed to his lips now.

"How's work?" Bram asked as they walked toward the Purcells' house.

"Good. I got a new assignment today. A pet store in Cheyenne."

Bram always tread lightly when asking about Zachary's job. It was clear that he valued the structure and schedule of work very much, and didn't enjoy it being interrupted or challenged. More frustrating, though, was his valorization of a company that clearly didn't value his artistic innovation just because it was prestigious. Bram knew that he'd been raised with a huge advantage: he'd never learned to esteem things just because they had cachet. In fact, he'd been raised to question what such value was based in. Spoiler alert: if you traced it back far enough, it was always either money or exclusivity. Usually both.

So when Zachary said things like "they're the premier architecture firm in the Midwest," what Bram heard was, "they make a lot of money and pay a lot of money so there's competition to work there." Which simply boiled down to *money = value*, an equation he just didn't subscribe to. And he didn't really think Zachary cared about money, beyond having enough to pay his rent and buy the art supplies that he used for his Halloween displays. So he was fairly sure that what Zachary actually valued was other people's estimation of his job. What he wasn't sure of yet was whether Zachary cared what people thought (he didn't seem to in most other contexts) or had simply internalized the message of what success looked like at an early age like so many people and was now living out the results.

The latter seemed far more likely to Bram, and he wondered if this performance of career success helped Zachary offset the varying degrees of negative feedback he got for his social demeanor.

He hadn't wanted to bring up any of this, even though Zachary so clearly wasn't happy doing all the boring projects that he got assigned, because he'd seemed offended when Bram had asked why he didn't look for a position that would value his creativity more.

So instead, he said, "That's cool. What kind of design does the pet store need?"

For a moment, there was a flare in Zachary's eyes and Bram could practically *see* the weird, fascinating creation that Zachary had dreamed up. But then it died, and he said, "It's a pretty basic design. The trick is figuring out how to maximize savings by designing a space that will minimize materials and still give the client the square footage they've requested."

It caused him nearly physical pain to watch Zachary's skills and creativity wasted on these boxes that anyone could design.

"Oh. Cool," was all Bram said.

Fortunately, they were approaching the Purcells' house, and Bram led them across the street, where he knelt beside Hemlock as if they were just paused to give her a little rest and sniff.

Mr. Purcell came out of the house, saw them, and waved. Bram and Zachary waved back, and Mr. Purcell made a show of flipping the switch on his Halloween lights and then lifting his hands as if he were god giving light to the world.

Only it wasn't his orange and black Halloween lights that went on—it was red and green Christmas lights.

Mr. Purcell stood frozen for a moment, looking utterly flummoxed. He looked up at the sky, as if searching for snow, and Bram could practically see him wondering if he'd lost three months and it actually *was* Christmas.

Then he spun in a circle, saw Bram and Zachary, and simply said, *"Hey!"*

Bram and Zachary dissolved into laughter, draping over one another. Hem nuzzled them both, delighted by this display.

"You—What did—How the hell did—*What?*" he sputtered.

Bram cleared his throat and they approached. From his pocket, Bram took a note and handed it to Mr. Purcell with ceremony.

"Your Halloween lights will be returned when you gift a neighbor with a lighthearted Halloween prank," Mr. Purcell read.

"I like that you added 'lighthearted,'" Zachary snorted.

The idea to turn his and Zachary's prank war into a chance for them to be a team had struck him the moment he saw the Purcells' lights. He'd been surprised that Zachary kept it going after they were… whatever they were—a couple? And he'd relished the chance to collaborate that the lights had presented, rather than having to say, *Hey, now that we're having sex and hanging out maybe we could stop pranking each other?*

"Well," Bram said, "a prank is fun if it's light-hearted. If it's mean then it's no fun at all."

For a moment it looked like Mr. Purcell might decide that none of this was fun. But then he looked around his yard at the Christmas lights in exactly the same places the Halloween lights were, as if they'd transformed overnight, and started to chuckle.

"Damn, how'd you boys pull that off?" Then he called, "Miriam, come out and take a look at this," and his wife poked her head out the door.

"At what?"

It seemed to take her a moment to realize the lights should've been a different color, and when she did realize, she grinned.

"I guess this means you owe me a Christmas present," she said brightly, then winked at Bram and went back inside.

Mr. Purcell held up the Halloween light ransom note, and said, "All right, I get it. Don't break the chain."

Then he, too, winked, saluted them, and walked next door, dragging his neighbors out to see the miracle of the color-changing lights.

"So," Zachary said. "You've lived here for five seconds and already started a neighborhood prank war. I hope you're proud."

"Excuse me. *You* started the neighborhood prank war when you dumped paint on Snaggletooth." That was the name he'd given his dragon in his head.

"That wasn't—I didn't mean to— Yeah, okay, fine."

Bram grinned at him and hooked his arm through Zachary's elbow. They continued down the street—

after all, Hem did need her walk—and when they got back to their own houses, Bram took a gamble.

"Don't suppose I could tempt you to come hang out at my place instead of going back to work for—" he checked the time "—one hour and six minutes?"

Zachary hesitated like maybe he was considering it, so Bram played his ace card.

"I'll show you how the cat boxes are coming along…"

Zachary bit at his lip and Bram could see the actual discomfort it caused him to contemplate not working his usual full day. He was just about to tell Zachary never mind, in fact, when Zachary blew out a breath and muttered, "Screw it. Yeah, okay," looking up at Bram.

Sunlight coursed through Bram. "Yeah? Yay!"

Something like a smile answered him on Zachary's face. It was uncertain and a little hesitant, like maybe he'd never known the joy of skipping school or sneaking in an extra-long lunch break. Or maybe, Bram mused, he couldn't believe that his presence and company would cause anyone excitement.

That was unacceptable. Bram squeezed Zachary to his side and led him through the front door.

Usually when they spent time together it was at Zachary's house. Bram knew his space was messier than Zachary enjoyed. But he'd straightened up that morning, hoping to make Zachary more comfortable there. Fortunately, since he didn't have a lot of stuff, the mess was easy to contain.

He was using the living room as his workspace, and he led Zachary inside.

The week before he'd gotten the logs—which were actually tree trunks—and hollowed them out in Charlie Matheson's woodworking studio. It was where he'd also cut all of the wood for the cat boxes that would go downtown.

Zachary immediately knelt to examine the boxes, running curious fingers over the hollowed-out tree trunks.

"These are larger than I'd imagined," he said. "But I can see that it's good to have them longer for warmth."

"Yeah, exactly. That's why I left one end closed too. So the wind wouldn't blow through. Plus with more than one cat in there it'd be warmer."

Zachary continued on to the in-town boxes.

"Is this for the Odeon?"

"Yeah. I talked to Henry and he was very into the idea. He said he'd put a donations box in the lobby too, where people can drop off cat food and blankets and stuff. Rye and Charlie helped him with the Odeon reno so he's happy to help out."

Bram was happy Zachary had noticed that one. It was his favorite. The shape echoed the Odeon's proscenium, with a red velvet curtain framing it. The entrance to the box was in the back with an offset piece to protect the opening from cold and wind that was shaped like a box of popcorn. It was large, since the theater had a large sidewalk in front of it—easily big enough for four or five cats to curl up, were they so inclined.

Bram had painted it the night before and the scent of paint still hung in the air.

"Want some help?" Zachary offered. He looked enthusiastically around the room.

"Sure. Do you want to paint the one for the coffee shop? It's all put together."

Zachary inspected it.

"You went with the spilling coffee—awesome," Zachary said, eyes bright.

"Yup. Can you see how it's supposed to go?"

Zachary nodded. He was, Bram realized, the last person he needed to help see structures that weren't quite there.

Hemlock flopped onto her cushion in the corner and Bram got out the paints.

"Do you want to borrow something so you don't get paint on your suit?"

Zachary looked down at his impeccable outfit like he'd forgotten what he was wearing.

"Yeah, thanks."

"You could just paint with no clothes, if you want," he said with a wink.

He'd been going for flirtatious, but Zachary said, "You're right."

He stripped out of his suit and hung it neatly over the back of a chair. Then, in his underwear, he picked up the paintbrush.

"Oh, jeez," Bram said, eyes magnetized to Zachary's lithe form. "That's…okay."

He was across the room in two strides and almost got a paintbrush in the nostril as he bent to kiss Zachary.

Zachary grinned at his ardor and let himself be caught up in Bram's arms, paintbrush falling to the floor.

Bram loved the feel of Zachary in his arms. He was small, but strong, and he held on so damn tight when Bram kissed him.

The kiss was deep, and a wave of heat broke over him, but Bram let him go with one last kiss to his cheek.

"You're very tempting," he said, and he thought he saw the slightest flush over Zachary's cheeks, but maybe it was just a trick of the light.

They painted in quiet companionship for about an

hour. Bram worked on the box for the library, smiling as he inked titles of books onto spines with a detail brush.

Cat on a Hot Tin Roof, *Cat's Eye*, *Cat's Cradle*, and *The Catcher in the Rye*.

Bram finished before Zachary and was able to watch his meticulous work. Zachary held the paintbrush like it was a pencil and used tiny, precise strokes.

From afar, the to-go cup looked like you could stop to pick it up and throw it away. The spill of wooden coffee that was the entry to the shelter looked wet.

"How did you learn to paint like this?" Bram asked, impressed.

Zachary shrugged.

"I always liked painting."

"You're amazing."

Zachary looked confused for a moment, then said, "Thank you. Should I put something on the cup? Like a name or an order?"

"Catnip Latte," Bram suggested.

Zachary nodded and lettered it onto the cup. His eyes were bright with interest.

"Can I ask you something?"

Zachary mmm-hmmed, eyes on his work.

"Do you like your job?"

"I love my job," he said instantly, still painting.

"Right, I know you love architecture. But do you like designing pet stores and other boxes that don't let you express your skill or creativity?"

Zachary's eyes darted left and then right.

"It's a good job. They aren't easy to get."

"I'm sure they're not," Bram allowed.

He'd decided to broach the topic, but clearly this

wasn't something Zachary was open to discussing. At least not right now.

"You want to do another one?" he asked instead.

Zachary took the bait.

"This one is for that bakery on the corner of Main and…"

"Turner," Zachary said. "Got it."

He studied the cutout, squinting. Bram had come up with this one himself.

"A giant croissant?"

"Yup." Bram was relieved it was recognizable.

Zachary smiled. "Okay, I can do that."

As soon as he started painting, it was like he went away somewhere, his essence retreating an inch inside his skin. Unreachable. He worked for an hour without speaking, not seeming to notice Bram starting and finishing the Matheson's Hardware shelter, washing his brushes, or taking a shower.

When Bram came to ask if he was hungry, he was crouching in front of the shelter examining his work.

It was golden brown and flaky-looking, and for some reason it struck Bram as one of the cutest things he'd ever seen —a cold cat curled up inside a giant croissant, warm from the oven.

"Damn, it's so good it's making me hungry," Bram said.

Zachary drew him close with a curled finger and Bram sank beside him. He pointed at the layers of pastry and when Bram squinted he saw that in several places the whorls of dough formed…

"Oh my god," he breathed. "Tiny cat faces. You freaksome genius."

Zachary laughed with joy.

"I realize it could be interpreted as a bit ghoulish—like the croissants are made out of kittens or something. But I didn't mean it that way. I thought maybe unconsciously the cats would recognize familiar patterns and be drawn to it. I don't know. I don't know how cats work. Just a thought."

Bram also could not claim to know how cats worked. But he was learning how Zachary Glass worked, and it was with utter, sincere dedication to every single detail.

Bram wasn't exactly sure why he found that so attractive and endearing, but he really, really did. In fact, there was a lot about his responses to Zachary that were surprising him. Bram had always been drawn to people that felt like his family: warm, socially skilled, and motivated to destroy the tethers of corporate capitalism that threatened to ensnare anyone not actively working against them.

When they'd first met, Zachary had seemed the opposite: standoffish, prickly, and so dedicated to the nine-to-five grind that he wore suits while working from his own living room.

How, Bram had wondered, was he drawn to this man? Of course, he'd quickly realized that Zachary wasn't standoffish, he just operated in tune to a different set of social mandates. He wasn't prickly, he'd just always had to defend his way of being in the world to detractors and had internalized it as a default. And he wasn't dedicated to the grind, he was soothed and supported by a strict schedule that freed his mind from the pressure of having to make certain choices so that it could meander freely through his creative process.

The resistance to seeing that his job wasn't a great fit for him…well, that was a conversation for another time.

"You hungry?" he asked, instead of gathering Zachary in his arms and telling him how much he delighted Bram.

"Yeah, actually. Painting this made me hungry."

Bram stood and offered Zachary a hand. He pulled him up easily and for a moment he thought Zachary was going to hug him, kiss him, something. But he just steadied himself and cleaned his brushes without comment before donning his clothes once more. Most people looked very different in a suit than they did in their underwear, but Zachary didn't. His demeanor didn't change at all.

Bram cooked them pasta with mushrooms and fresh herbs and when he passed Zachary a steaming bowl, Zachary held it for a moment like he was Oliver Twist or something.

"What?"

Zachary shook his head.

"I just don't remember the last time someone cooked for me." He paused, then said, "My mom, I guess."

"Was she a good cook?"

"I don't know. I always ate it, but..." He shrugged and Bram took that to mean *You know I don't care about food*.

They sat at Bram's newly constructed kitchen table to eat. Zachary took a few bites of pasta and said, "It's good, thanks."

Bram narrowed his eyes at him, and he laughed. "Fine, it's totally edible, I don't care about it, but I was being polite because I appreciate you doing the work of cooking it. Okay? Better?"

And actually, it was.

Bram wouldn't have thought that he'd prefer to hear someone say they didn't care what his cooking tasted like, but the more time he spent around Zachary, the more he found himself soothed and reassured by his particular blunt variety of honesty.

It would be easy to say it was because after Naveen and Drake he would prefer *any* kind of honesty to any kind of lie, but it wasn't that simple.

It wasn't just the feeling that Zachary was being truthful. It was that his truths came without judgment. Like he detached facts from any evaluative metric, so he was able to tell them easily and without struggle. He didn't assign any value to "tasting the food" so telling Bram he didn't care about it was a logical extension, not a confession.

Bram's phone started vibrating with texts from multiple siblings.

"Oh, shoot, it's family Skype tonight. I forgot."

"Okay, I'll get out of your way." Zachary started to clear his bowl.

"No, wait!" Bram suddenly, desperately wanted Zachary to stay. To be a part of his life. "Sorry, didn't mean to shout. Just, I'd love it if you wanted to meet everyone. I've talked all about you so they're dying to meet you."

"You've talked about me?"

Zachary said it slowly, like he couldn't quite imagine it.

"Of course."

Bram didn't clarify that his siblings had sent him *dozens* of texts begging for private introductions, pictures, and details about Zachary.

"Okay," Zachary said quietly. He sat back down and

patted himself into shape though he was already immaculate except for his wayward curls, which sproinged joyously.

"Yeah? Awesome."

Bram sat next to him on the bench and propped his phone on the bookstand he used for a phone stand.

Before he signed on, he pressed a kiss to Zachary's cheek. Zachary turned wide eyes on him, but leaned in and kissed him sweetly.

"Do I have food in my teeth?" he asked, then bared them.

"Nope, you're good. Me?"

Bram did the same and Zachary reached over and brushed something off his lip.

"Thanks," Bram breathed. It had been an intimate gesture and it had made his stomach go all squishy.

"Um. Brace yourself, I guess?" he said as he clicked the *join call* button.

"Huh?" Zachary asked.

Chapter Sixteen

Zachary

The screen came alive with faces and voices. Zachary knew Bram had four siblings, but he had no reference for what a seven-person family was like. One of them was cooking dinner, another was outside, a third had two kids jammed into view, and the fourth seemed to be upside down. Then there were the parents, who were pressed close together to share a screen. But before Zachary could track what they were talking about, one by one, all eyes snapped to the cameras and they started talking at once.

"Bram!" and "Is that Zachary?" and "HELLO, BRAM'S FRIEND!" and "About time, you little sneak."

Next to him, Bram cleared his throat and when Zachary turned to him, he was turning red, flushing from his throat to the apples of his cheeks.

"Are you okay?" Zachary asked.

"Mmm-hmm," Bram answered, strangled. "Just, maybe this was a bad idea." But before he could say anything more, their mother held up her hand and the other feeds went quiet.

"Wow," Zachary said. "I can't believe that worked."

"Bram, would you like to introduce your guest?" his mother said. "Kids, can you introduce yourselves too?"

She said it casually, but there was an air of steel in her voice. Zachary only had time to be amused at referring to these adults in the twenties and thirties as "kids," including one brother who appeared to be even larger than Bram, before Bram spoke.

"Hi, everyone. This is Zachary Glass. He's just been helping me paint the cat shelters I told you about, and I wanted you to meet him. Please be humans instead of jackals. Thank you."

"Zachary, it's very nice to meet you. I'm Mirabelle, Bram's mother."

"I'm Bram's dad," the older man said. "Trent."

The brother who seemed even bigger than Bram waved. He was the one cooking dinner and he'd paused his activities.

"Hey, Zachary. I'm Thistle. I'm the oldest of this wolf pack. Nice to meet you."

"Zachary, hi! I'm Vega, the youngest sister." She smiled a sweet, wide smile that put Zachary at ease. He waved.

"Omigod, *finally*!" the upside-down sister said, then her screen tipped queasily, and she was right-side up.

"I'm Moon, one of Bram's younger sisters, and I can't help but notice that you're—"

A hand came from behind her and clapped over

her mouth, silencing her. The person belonging to the hand ducked into view and rested her chin on Moon's shoulder.

"Hi, Larkspurs," she said. They clearly knew her. "Zachary, I'm Ming, Moon's girlfriend, and I would like to apologize for whatever is almost assuredly going to come out of my beloved's enormous, rude mouth during the tenure of this call." She grinned. Zachary grinned back at her and smoothed down his shirt.

The final sister, who was on mute and talking to her kids, unmuted and said, "Hey, Zachary. I'm Birch. These small monsters are Millie and Dorothy. Nice to meet you."

Then everyone was silent, and Zachary saw his face in the camera, blinking at them all. Bram put a warm palm on his back and slid it up and down his spine. You couldn't see it on camera, and it made Zachary think about all the things that could be going on in the back of all the other people's cameras that he couldn't see.

"Hi," he said. "I'm Zachary." Then, compelled to use the same format as they all had, he added, "I'm Bram's… Halloween prank war nemesis?"

The Larkspur family smiled, laughed, nodded enthusiastically, looked wryly, and nodded, respectively.

"Welcome," one of them said, though Zachary couldn't tell which one.

Zachary called his mom for the first time in two months. She'd left him several messages over the last few weeks, which he'd ignored. But seeing Bram's family, so close and so joyful at one another's company, had made him pick up the phone.

"Zacky!" she answered. The sound of her voice wound his stomach like spaghetti on a fork.

"Hi, Mom."

He didn't say "How are you?" because that was always an invitation for her to start talking about the case.

Not that not asking usually avoided it.

"Your father's been having terrible reflux lately," she said. "So he's taking a new medication."

She talked for several minutes about his father's health and her friend Joanie, whom Zachary had never met and wasn't entirely convinced actually existed since his mother's relationship with her seemed to revolve entirely around Zumba and smoothies.

"I'm up for a promotion at work," Zachary said. "I fly to Denver for the interview next week. If I get it, I'll be the youngest person ever to hold the position."

"That's wonderful," his mother said. "Congratulations."

"Well, I didn't get it yet," he said.

"I'm sure you will, sweetie."

Zachary began to sweat.

"No, it's not guaranteed. It will be competitive," he said. That wasn't quite right, but he didn't know how else to say it. She was congratulating him like it was nothing—a done deal, a guarantee—and it was notable, significant, a standout. Making it sound guaranteed stripped the achievement from it.

"Well, if they're smart, they'll pick you," she repeated.

Zachary sighed.

"Listen, I need your help with something," his mother said. In the space of one sentence, she'd shifted completely into the intensity that Zachary knew so well.

Suddenly he wished he'd never called.

"There's movement with your sister's case. I've been contacted by someone who worked as a waitress in a diner sixty miles east of here. She guarantees that your sister came in three days in a row and was meeting someone. So I need you to go to the diner and ask for Sharon Barklee. Barklee—with two Es. And then put up flyers all around Riverton. You can design them, right, honey? Like you did before? You're so much better at it than me."

"Mom, Mom. I can't go to Riverton. I work. I have a job. I'm going to Denver."

"You can go after work. It's a 24-hour diner."

A familiar tornado of exhaustion and frustration swept Zachary up. This was the fifth or sixth person in the last ten years who had claimed to see Sarah. And of course they did, because his mother kept advertising a reward for a sighting of her.

The first time it had happened had only been a year after they moved to Garnet Run, and even Zachary had gotten his hopes up, despite thinking he'd resigned himself to Sarah's permanent absence.

Things happened. People left and came back. You never knew. Sarah was young and maybe she'd changed her mind. He'd gotten caught up in it all, just like his parents had. When it proved to be nothing, he'd felt like he was grieving all over again. But the next time it had happened, he'd known better.

But his mother had been sure the next time too. And the time after that. Every time she was sure, because she didn't have anything else to be and keep living one day after the next. He didn't want to take that away from her, but he'd been done helping her sustain it years ago.

"Mom," he said, as gently as he could. "Sarah wasn't at that diner. That waiter didn't see her. I'm not going to Riverton. I'm sorry. Can we talk about something else?"

"You could go on a weekend," she continued, her voice taking on the steel edge of someone who would have her will done and pity anyone who got in her way. "It would be a nice Saturday drive. You could get some pie at the diner, talk to Sharon, and put up the flyers. It's lovely out."

"I'm sorry, but I'm not going. You need to ask someone else."

His mother started in again, and her inability to be reasoned with infuriated Zachary. This conversation was over.

"I'm going to hang up now, Mom. I love you."

Then Zachary ended the call and lay down on the floor with his eyes closed, trying to scrape her voice out of his brain.

"A haunted hayride?"

"Yeah!" Bram stood in Zachary's doorway, dressed in denim and flannel, looking like he should be doing something with hay himself.

"Why?"

Bram wrinkled his brow.

"Um, because it's fun and seasonal and awesome?"

"Well, it beats driving sixty miles to ask a waiter about my dead sister's ghost," Zachary muttered.

"What?"

"Nothing. Um, yeah, okay."

"Great!"

Bram stepped inside and folded Zachary into a full-body hug.

It was quickly becoming one of Zachary's favorite things. Being completely surrounded by Bram's warm, muscular body made him feel safe and cared for. He nuzzled his face tighter against Bram and breathed in his sunny smell.

"Mmm," Bram hummed, and stroked up and down his spine. Then he worked his fingers at the nape of Zachary's neck and into his hair, and Zachary melted. Bram took his weight easily.

"Don't stop," Zachary said into Bram's chest.

"What?" Bram asked, but he followed the instruction anyway, so Zachary didn't repeat it.

After several minutes of cuddling and petting, Zachary felt like a recharged battery.

"You okay?" Bram asked.

Zachary nodded.

"Okay, then get your coat!"

"Oh, you meant...now?"

"Yeah! It's a Saturday in October, we've gotta do Halloween-y things!"

"Oh. Okay."

For all that Zachary loved horror movies and loved designing and executing his Halloween decorations, he'd never pursued Halloween-y activities. But it did sound fun. Especially if Bram was going to be with him.

Yeah. Definitely better than talking to a waiter about his dead sister's ghost.

The thing about riding on Bram's motorcycle was that it made the getting there part just as much of an event as the being there part. The cold air kissed Zachary's face and his clothes snapped around him like the wind was trying to pull him inside it. The familiar countryside whipped past at a new speed, the autumn leaves blurring to dappled color and light.

They pulled into a farm about twenty miles away and Bram helped Zachary off the bike. He felt expansive and oxygenated, like a drink fizzing over the top of the glass.

The sky around them was huge, and the air smelled of sweet decomposition and apples. Autumn in an orchard. Zachary hadn't experienced it since he was a child.

Bram grabbed his hand and interlaced their fingers, excitedly pulling him toward the sign for the hayrides.

A pumpkin patch to their right promised perfect pumpkins for carving, and the orchard to their left promised perfect apples for bobbing—not that Zachary would ever bob for apples; it was horribly unsanitary.

So they had that whole Halloween vibe nailed.

Mostly, though, Zachary paid attention to the feel of Bram's warm hand in his, since apparently they were holding hands now.

They passed a scarecrow with straw leaking from between the buttons of its shirt.

"Hey, you're twins," Zachary said, pointing. The scarecrow's plaid flannel was a shade darker blue than Bram's but otherwise identical. It wore blue jeans as well.

Bram chuckled and let go of Zachary's hand to stand with an arm slung around the scarecrow.

"Take a picture for my family?" he asked.

Zachary pulled out his phone. He took several shots that displayed their matching outfits fully. Then, almost before he realized he was doing it, he zoomed in on Bram's smiling face, and snapped a picture just for himself. A picture to prove to himself that he had the attention and care of this glorious man—at least for a little while.

Then he deleted the picture because it felt creepy to take it without Bram's permission.

He sent the pics of Bram and the scarecrow to Bram's phone and Bram sent a group text that popped up on Zachary's phone.

Found my soul mate, the text said, and for a moment, Zachary's heart leapt into his throat. But then he realized it was referring to the scarecrow, obviously.

A flood of messages pinged in Zachary's phone, all from numbers he didn't know.

A raised eyebrow emoji, a laughing emoji, a GIF from *The Wicker Man*, which made Zachary have a favorite sibling of Bram's even if he didn't know which one it was.

"Um," Zachary said. He held up his phone.

"Oh, uh. Should I not have included you?"

Bram's cheeks pinked. Zachary could tell he meant it to be something nice, but he didn't really have any interest in a bunch of random texts from people he didn't know.

"It's nice," Zachary said carefully. "But also very distracting if they keep writing."

"Got it," Bram said. He got a message then that said, END.

"Does that make them stop?"

"Yep. Sibling code." Bram winked.

Zachary wasn't sure that using the word *end* to ask

people to end a conversation quite counted as code, but he appreciated its efficacy nonetheless.

"Okay, ready?" Bram asked, excitement firmly back in place.

"I guess so."

They queued up with families and young couples near a fleet of tractors pulling wagons. Hay bales were stacked along the edges for people to sit on. When Bram and Zachary were waved into a wagon, Zachary squirmed to find a comfortable way to sit, but the hay was pokey and itched through his pants.

Bram slid off his jacket.

"Stand up."

He put the jacket down on the hay, and when Zachary sat down again, the itchiness was gone.

"Won't you be cold?"

"Warm-blooded."

"Thanks."

Bram put his arm around Zachary's back. One of the boys sitting across from them with his family kept staring at them. Zachary's stomach tightened. Was the kid going to say something? He reminded himself that when it happened he shouldn't tell the kid to shut up because that would make his parents mad and it had been a long time since Zachary got in a fight, but he was pretty sure in a moving hayride would be a pretty unpleasant place to take it up again.

Fortunately, once they started moving, there were other things to draw the kid's attention.

They drove through a wooden cutout arch that announced they were now entering a haunted field.

"Shouldn't we be doing this at night?" Zachary asked, confused.

Bram bit his lip.

"Um. I thought it would be too scary at night," he whispered haltingly.

Zachary smiled, incredibly endeared.

"Well, I hope you and all the six-year-olds have a great time," he teased.

Bram chuckled warmly and gave him a friendly noogie.

The "haunted" part of the hayride mainly consisted of people in masks jumping out from behind stacks of hay bales on the ground. They were clearly keeping it G-rated for the family crowd (and Bram).

Zachary entertained himself by mentally editing the hayride into something truly scary. He was about to tell Bram about how he'd execute a particular effect when the man in question grabbed his hand and squeaked.

A person in a clown mask had just jumped out from behind a tree.

Bram blew out a breath and calmed himself.

"You okay?"

Bram turned wide eyes the color of the autumn sky on Zach and blinked. "This is scary," he asserted.

Zachary patted his hand and decided he shouldn't share his specially edited scary edition of the hayride with Bram, even in broad daylight.

The hayride did have one neat effect. As they approached the end of the ride, passing through a twin wooden cutout arch to the one at the beginning, the whole trailer let out a collective sigh of relief. And just as they were doing so, three different masked people jumped out from behind the arch and shot them with silly string.

Several people screamed, the kid who'd been staring at them earlier jumped up, and Bram leapt over the side of the cart to the ground, and ran toward the orchard.

"Er. Excuse me," Zachary said as he stepped over people's feet to get to the back of the car.

He jumped down and followed Bram, who had his hands resting on his thighs, panting.

"You okay?"

"Oh my *god*!" Bram said, wide-eyed. He grabbed Zachary and hugged him close like a stuffed animal after a nightmare.

"That one *really* got me," he said.

Zachary stroked his back and slid his hand into Bram's. A strange sensation lodged somewhere between his throat and his stomach. A fluttery warmth that seemed to intensify every time Bram squeezed his hand or smiled in his direction.

Chapter Seventeen

Bram

Zachary went about choosing a pumpkin with intent seriousness. Bram didn't know exactly what he was looking for, but he supposed Zachary would know it when he saw it.

For the moment, Bram was happy to trail after him as he subjected the pumpkins to scrutiny.

It had been a long time since Bram had felt like this—at the beginning of something that he knew, deep inside, in the place that even the recent hit to his confidence couldn't shake, was significant.

He and Drake had been a whirlwind at the beginning. Bram had been smitten and their chemistry had been undeniable. He'd thrown himself into the relationship with everything he was and planned their future.

He'd imagined the two of them having what his parents had: a partnership of love and support and mutual caring that could weather anything the world threw their way.

After the breakup, when Bram was at his lowest, staying in Moon's guest room and crying into her oatmeal, he had realized something. He hadn't been making plans for a future with Drake. He had been making plans for *his* future and he had cast Drake in the role of his partner.

He'd taken that epiphany to Moon, who had blinked at him slowly and said, "Yup."

But although it had apparently been clear to her (and his parents, it was later revealed), Bram hadn't seen it. And it made him wonder how much else of his relationship with Drake he hadn't seen either.

Nothing with Zachary Glass had been a whirlwind. In fact, Bram had the sense that if a whirlwind tried to sweep Zachary up, he'd scowl at it and say, *I do not have a whirlwind in my schedule for today, goodbye.*

Bram snorted at the image.

"What?" the man in question asked.

"What are you looking for?"

"The perfect pumpkin," Zachary said, as if that should have been apparent.

"What makes a pumpkin perfect?"

Zachary blinked at him. The question seemed to irritate him. Bram put up his hands and let Zachary go back to his search.

After a few more minutes, Zachary stood up and crossed his arms, hugging himself.

"Can't find the perfect one?" Bram asked.

"There are too many to look at to definitively render a judgment," Zachary said mournfully.

"What happens if you pick the wrong one?"

"Nothing *happens*, it'll just irritate me."

He sounded huffy and irritated already, and he scanned the offending field of thousands of pumpkins.

Bram stepped close and put his hands on Zachary's shoulders.

"What if *all* the pumpkins are actually perfect and your criteria are what's flawed?" Bram asked gently.

Zachary's scowl deepened but he was listening.

"The shape and density of the flesh determine what you carve from them. It's just like whittling. You get a piece of wood and it tells you what it can be. Sure, it might not be able to be *anything*, but part of the art is letting the natural form determine what you create from it."

Zachary was listening intently.

"Like designing a structure on an uncleared plot of land."

Bram nodded.

"Did you pick one?" Zachary asked.

Bram scanned the ground around them and saw a twisted, oblong pumpkin with one side flattened and scarred. He plucked it off the ground.

"Got it."

Zachary narrowed his eyes. "Now you're just showing off."

Bram laughed. "Yup."

"I can't *believe* with all your Halloween decoration enthusiasm and unchallenged forty-eight-year winning streak or whatever it is that you never carve pumpkins!"

They were back at Bram's house and had decided

to carve pumpkins in the living room, since the floor was already covered for the shelter painting.

"They make bad decorations because they rot," Zachary said, as if contributing to his decor vision was the only thing anything could be useful for.

"Do you even *like* Halloween?" Bram asked. "I assumed you did because of the decorations and how much you love horror movies, but would you have the same enthusiasm for this competition if we lived on, I dunno, Cupid Road and this were a Valentine's Day decoration contest?"

Zachary contemplated this.

"I would still participate. I would still enjoy designing a decoration scheme, although I don't think Valentine's Day provides quite as wide a range of possibilities for decor. But I do like Halloween."

He chewed at his lip, lost in thought.

"I used to love dressing up. When I was ten I went as a geodesic dome and Sarah went as Buckminster Fuller. No one knew what we were."

He said it wistfully, so Bram did his best to swallow the bark of laughter at a ten-year-old Zachary dressed as a geodesic dome.

"Did your sister like Halloween too?"

"She loved it. And horror movies. Witches, vampires, anything supernatural or spooky. She's the one who showed me my first horror movies. I was so freaked out. I was maybe eight or nine and she was twelve or thirteen. My parents were out for dinner and she was in charge. She put on this movie *Blood Mansion* that she really loved. And I was, like, hiding under the blanket, watching through a worn spot."

Bram shuddered at the idea.

"How'd you get from there to liking them?"

Zachary absently separated pumpkin seeds from the wet guts. He was wearing gloves because he didn't like the feel of the wet pumpkin innards.

"When you're scared, you can't pay attention. Being scared takes up your whole body and mind. But Sarah would point at the screen and say, 'That's a light on a film set,' and 'The actor is covered in corn syrup and food dye—I bet a shower feels good at the end of work.' She'd point out that the music was getting more tense because the director wanted us to get scared. And after a few movies, I could see it too. It was like she'd shown me the code of how the whole genre worked and once I realized it was to make me feel a certain way, I could choose whether I wanted to feel that way or just think about it. It let me pay attention to more than just being scared. To the camera angles and the music, the lighting and the sound design."

Zachary's voice had gone slow and soft, like he was talking to himself.

"Do you want to know a secret?" he asked.

Bram had never wanted to know someone's secrets more than he wanted to know Zachary's.

"Yes."

"For the first couple months after she disappeared, I thought maybe she was playing a joke on me. There was this one movie we loved, about a girl who fakes her own death to get away from her life but then ends up getting killed for real. Every morning when I woke up I thought for sure there would be a message from her letting me know that she was safe and had gotten away from Wyoming. I thought one day I'd go see a movie and the credits would start and it would say 'directed by Sarah Glass,' and I would know that she was okay. I even texted her to say that if she gave me a clue I wouldn't tell our parents."

Bram's heart hurt. It was so clear that his sister's disappearance had deeply traumatized Zachary.

"What are you going to do?"

"Huh?" Bram asked, deep in thoughts about Zachary's sister.

"On your pumpkin. What are you going to carve?"

"Oh, I don't know yet."

He examined it, turning it to see all sides. Then he took his pocketknife and began to cut.

Zachary watched for a few minutes, then returned to contemplating his own pumpkin. Bram lost himself in the carving, the flesh of the pumpkin giving way much easier than the wood he was accustomed to.

Halloween when he was a kid was a blur of siblings and lost pieces of homemade costumes, running through the neighborhood, and at least one sibling (usually him) ending the night in tears. The next morning, they'd wake and find it November and the subtle slide into a Washington State winter would begin. Before you knew it, it was winter solstice, then Christmas, and Halloween was long forgotten.

His mind wandered to what it would have been like if one of them had disappeared. But it was like a toothache that his tongue shied away from. He didn't even want to let himself linger on the thought.

"Hey, that's…that's my house."

Bram looked down at the pumpkin he was carving. "Yep."

"But that's not Halloween-y."

Bram shrugged. "Does it have to be?"

"I assumed."

Bram looked at Zachary's pumpkin. Into it, he had carved…

"You carved a pumpkin in your pumpkin?"

"Well. Yes."

Bram wanted to fold Zachary in his arms and kiss the hell out of him, but he was slimy with pumpkin guts and knew Zachary wouldn't appreciate that.

"That's just…so damn cute."

"Why?"

"I don't know, it just is. You're cute."

Zachary accepted that answer with a shrug, but Bram thought he looked pleased.

They cleaned up the pumpkin guts and made sure the jack-o'-lanterns were out of Hemlock's reach.

Zachary peeled his gloves off and sniffed at his hands with distaste.

"Do you want to take a shower?"

Zachary nodded with relief.

"Um. What would you think of me taking one with you?"

Zachary's eyes got wide for a moment, then he smiled and nodded.

They watched each other undress and stepped beneath the hot water. Bram inclined his head and caught Zachary's mouth in a kiss. He adored how Zachary kissed, hungry and sweet, passionate and gentle, all at the same time.

They kissed hot and wet as the water poured over them. Zachary looked vulnerable and gorgeous with his wet hair dripping in his eyes and his mouth swollen from kisses.

"You're so beautiful," Bram murmured.

Something shifted in Zachary's face. A frown? No. Confusion. Then, maybe, delight?

Zachary plastered himself to Bram and kissed him all over again.

These kisses were hot and urgent, and Bram's body responded. They got out of the shower touching everywhere and only dried off hastily before kissing their way to the bed.

Bram lay down and ran a hand from Zachary's throat to his cock.

"What do you want, baby? Anything you want."

Zachary was flushed with heat and lust and all he seemed able to say was, "I want you."

Whatever that meant, Bram's sentiment was the same.

"I'm yours. Whatever you want."

Zachary straddled his thigh and kissed Bram's throat greedily. The sucking sent his blood boiling and shock waves through him.

Zachary inched down and sucked and bit at Bram's nipple. When his teeth closed around the tip, Bram arched off the bed.

Zachary grinned wolfishly. He kissed down Bram's ribs and up to the tender skin under his arms. He was a flame, catching in all the important places.

When he had Bram moaning, Zachary opened the drawer in the side table. He pulled out lube and a condom and held them up in question.

"Yes," Bram said. "Whatever you want."

Zachary's eyes burned, all intensity and want, and Bram wasn't sure what he was going to choose until he felt warm slickness slide inside him.

Zachary's fingers undulated, making him groan and spread his legs wider.

Zachary watched him as he explored. Every time Bram gasped or moaned, he redoubled his efforts on that spot, until his fingertips found the place that made Bram's vision go white.

Bram groaned as waves of pleasure spiraled through him, and Zachary hummed low in his throat with appreciation.

"Ready?" he asked, voice husky and eyelids at half-mast.

Bram nodded. It had been a long time, but he wanted Zachary fiercely.

Zachary slid inside him slowly, heat and steel and velvet, filling him up perfectly. Bram bit his lip against the temporary discomfort, then it dissolved into perfect fullness.

"Are you okay?" Zachary asked, frozen above him.

Bram nodded. "I'm great. You feel amazing."

Zachary moved slowly at first, seeking the angle that would replicate his fingers' pleasure. When he found it, Bram shuddered and clutched at his shoulders.

"That's so good, baby."

Zachary took that information and deployed it to fuck Bram to pieces.

Every time Bram thought the pleasure was plateauing, Zachary would slide that tiny bit deeper and awaken nerve endings that stoked the inferno. When the rhythm became comfortable, he'd slow down so Bram felt friction in every inch, then he'd speed up, snapping his hips to explode fireworks deep inside Bram.

Bram was so on edge that he ached, desperate for

release but unwilling to sacrifice a moment of the perfection that was Zachary Glass.

"Please, please, please," Bram heard himself beg.

"Touch yourself," Zachary breathed. His cheeks were flushed and he moved above Bram like a god.

The second Bram closed his hand around his aching erection, he gasped and swore, overloaded with pleasure.

It built and built until Bram didn't think he could take it anymore.

"Oh god, oh god, oh god," he chanted, straining for release.

Zachary changed his angle slightly and Bram cried out. It was perfect—so perfect, so damn perfect.

Each slide inside him brought him closer, and the gathering pleasure felt like it would explode into a supernova any moment.

When Zachary reached up and pinched his nipple, the jolt pushed him over the edge. Ecstasy overflowed and poured through him like molten silver, bowing his back and tightening every muscle.

The orgasm took him apart, and as it waned, Zachary threw his head back and came with a groan.

His weight fell forward, and Bram closed his arms around him. They lay that way for a minute, both breathing heavily. Bram felt blown apart, so satisfied and connected that he didn't want the moment ever to end. From Zachary's grip on him, he felt the same.

"That was amazing," Bram said softly, stroking Zachary's hair. He felt Zachary nod in agreement.

They lay there for another minute, before Zachary seemed to realize they were getting stuck together and moved.

He cast a hot glance at Bram before going into the bathroom.

"Jesus Christ," Bram said as he let himself stretch and luxuriate in how good he felt.

Zachary came back with a towel and a glass of water. He held both up uncertainly and Bram's heart swelled.

"Thank you."

Zachary stood by the bed still.

"Can we take another shower?"

This time, the shower was slow and liquid, all soft words and slick heat and long kisses.

Bram felt underwater, limbs and thoughts moving at the pleasure-drugged speed of a kiss.

"Thank you," Zachary said, and Bram nodded, continuing to wash Zachary's hair.

But Zachary turned around. "For letting me, um… I…"

He'd never seen Zachary look flustered over something before.

"Fuck me?" Bram rumbled into Zachary's ear, evoking a shudder and a nod. "It was my pleasure, I assure you."

Zachary shook his head. "Good. I just meant… thank you for not assuming that I would want…that just because…"

Bram wondered how many ignorant people had assumed that just because Zachary happened to be small that he would always want to bottom.

He rolled his eyes. "Of course. Whatever you want. I'm, uh, I'm pretty happy with whatever."

Zachary studied him intently. "Yeah. Yeah, you are, aren't you."

But before Bram could bristle at the dark undertone in Zachary's voice, Zachary said, "I'm glad," and kissed him so sweetly that Bram didn't have room left for anything but happiness.

"Stay?" he asked, and Zachary nodded.

They slipped beneath the covers and Zachary fit so perfectly in his arms that Bram was asleep before he knew it.

Chapter Eighteen

Zachary

The plane rode above the clouds as the sun rose, streaks of color appearing as if by a painter's hand. Zachary watched the journey to Denver out the window as he replayed the other night in his head over and over.

By the time they touched down in Colorado, he had come to two conclusions.

Number one: he really, really liked a man named Bramble Larkspur.

And number two: it was really, really going to hurt when he left.

"What are you doing in Colorado?" the woman next to him asked.

"Job interview."

"Oh. Good luck!"

"Thanks."

"I'm here to visit my daughter and my grandson. Would you like to see some pictures?"

"No, thank you," he said politely.

The woman sniffed as if he were being rude and Zachary pretended he was still held tight in Bram's arms, Bram's breath ruffling his hair.

The interview, Zachary thought, had gone well. Moray and Fisk had seemed impressed by his consistent output, his work ethic, and his loyalty to the company, and when he'd described the benefits of a robust morning routine, Elmer Moray had raised an eyebrow and said he'd have to think about that.

They'd had an assistant get him coffee and sparkling water, and now she was giving him a brief driving tour of Denver on the way back to drop him at the airport.

She described the nightlife, the sports opportunities, and the easy access to the region's natural beauty.

"Do you like working in the office?" Zachary asked.

"Oh, yeah. It's the top firm in the region. Everyone's really talented. Well, you know, I guess. You already work for them. But it's great to be around so many people working in the field on a daily basis."

Zachary nodded.

"Do you ski?" she asked.

"Nope."

"Oh. Well. Great skiing here."

The city unfolded before them, full of possibilities and unknowns.

"And, um, you know, weed's legal here, if that's

something you care about," she added into the silence. Then immediately, "Oh, god, don't tell them I said that."

"I won't. What is the social climate like for queer people here?"

"Oh. Uh. Fine, I think? I don't know about, like, clubs and stuff…"

"Never mind," Zachary said. "I'm ready to go to the airport now."

He was home by dinnertime the same day, almost as if he'd never left, fatigue the only evidence. Fatigue and a question: if he got the promotion, what would it be like to move from Garnet Run? To live in Denver?

Zachary was at his capacity for questions for the day, so he put on *Blood Mansion* and lay down on the couch. If he closed his eyes, he could almost imagine he was still soaring above the clouds, suspended in an infinite between.

Chapter Nineteen

Bram

Rye loved the shelters.

He'd gone with Bram to install them in town, dropping off boxes for those who wanted to collect donations of cat food, blankets, and towels. To a person, every shopkeeper had been in awe of the shelter designed to match their business.

A deep sense of satisfaction settled in Bram's stomach at the thought of being able to be helpful again.

He knocked on Zachary's door.

"Hi!" he said when Zachary opened it. "Guess what?"

Zachary stepped aside to let him in.

"Rye and I just dropped off all the cat shelters and everyone loved them—especially the ones you painted.

You're so damn good! And then we went around placing the hollow stump ones. Rye said they're great, so well done, you. And we wrote down where we put them so that next year we can see if they need to be resealed. And so we can clean them and stuff. Anyway, thanks for your help!"

Zachary smiled. "I'm glad. I hope the cats like them as much as the people."

"Do you like cats?" Bram asked. "Do you like animals? I never got the sense you were a dog fan, anyway."

Zachary was always absently respectful of Hemlock's presence, but didn't seek her out or pet her.

"No. I don't like them as something I would have responsibility for because I don't like being interrupted. But I like that they exist in the world. I like to watch them. Wes has a lot of animals, but his are all quiet, which I enjoy."

Bram couldn't even imagine how much training it would take to make all your animals quiet.

"Tarantulas are extremely interesting animals," Zachary went on absently.

Bram laughed. Only Zachary would lump tarantulas in with cats and dogs.

"And guess what?" Bram continued, too excited to keep the news to himself any longer. He'd begun to call Moon or his mom to tell them, like he usually would, but then he'd realized that the person he really wanted to tell was Zachary.

"Do you actually want me to guess?" Zachary asked sincerely.

It sent a spike of tenderness through Bram's guts.

"Nah, that's okay. I can just tell you." Bram glanced toward the couch. Sometimes Zachary didn't sit down until Bram did, happy to just talk standing up. But he saw the movie paused on the TV.

"Sorry, I didn't even ask if I was interrupting you."

"That's okay. I've seen it before. I paused it."

Bram sat on the couch and Zachary settled beside him, facing him instead of the TV.

"After we dropped off the shelters, Rye offered me a job." Bram grinned. "He started a catch and release program for neutering and spaying cats that were going to stay outdoors, but he and River—that's his coworker—"

"I know River. They're Adam's sibling."

"Oh! Got it. I'm still learning the genealogy of Garnet Run. Yeah, so River was going to help Rye with it, but they have their hands full with doing all the social media stuff and the daily cat care, so it didn't really get fully launched. So I'm going to run it. It's going to be so great. I'll get to be outside, I'll get to work with animals, and maybe if the project goes well, we'll even expand it. I don't know. Probably I'm getting ahead of myself. But Rye's so great, and so is River, and I'm really excited!"

He was trying very hard not to grab Zachary and bounce him up and down in excitement. His siblings were used to it—the way his enthusiasm sometimes felt larger than his body, uncontainable, but other people didn't always love being (as his father had called it) Tigger bounced.

"That's wonderful. Rye was smart to ask you—you'll do a great job."

He smiled, but there was something a tinge off about it.

"Are you okay? You look really tired."

Now that Bram looked, Zachary had darkness smudged under his eyes and his hair was wilder than he usually liked it to be.

Zachary nodded. "I am."

"How come, baby?"

Zachary's eyes widened at the endearment. It had come out so naturally and upon reflection it sounded right.

"Is it okay that I called you that?"

Zachary ducked his head and nodded. Bram had called him that during sex from time to time, but he hadn't been sure he noticed he was doing it.

"I like it."

"Me too."

He held an arm out to Zachary, who settled against his chest. He wound one of Zachary's curls around his finger.

"I went to Denver today."

It took Bram a moment to parse that. "Denver, Colorado?"

"Yeah. I'm up for a promotion and the interview was in person. The firm is in Denver."

Bram searched his mind for any mention of a promotion or a trip and found none.

Flustered, he said, "How did it go?"

"I think... I think it went well. I can't always tell about interpersonal things, though."

"Er, if you get the job, would you be moving to Denver?"

Zachary nodded. "Yes, the junior partners all work locally."

Bram blinked. "Oh. I... I didn't realize."

Thoughts ran riot through his head. Zachary leaving, Zachary not even telling him about a promotion that meant he might be leaving... Were they not in a relationship? Bram was pretty sure they were.

"I didn't mention it," Zachary confirmed. "I don't know if I'll get it."

"But if you get it, you'll take it?"

Zachary furrowed his brow. "Yes."

He looked so tired.

Bram stroked Zachary's back. Zachary drooped with a sigh of comfort and Bram leaned back, pretty sure Zachary would be asleep within minutes. Bram wanted to text Moon, but he wasn't sure what to say. *If your boyfriend moves without telling you, is that a sign he's just not that into you?*

As Zachary's eyes began to flutter closed, Bram asked, "Can I change what I assume is a terrifying movie to something else?"

"Mmm-hmm."

Zachary nudged the remote to him.

Bram put on a cheery baking show and half watched it while he stroked Zachary's hair and back, with Zachary's head in his lap.

"Go to sleep, baby," he murmured, and Zachary nodded, snuggling closer.

He slid his phone out to send Moon *not* that text. He thought Zachary had fallen asleep when he murmured softly.

"Do you ski?"

* * *

Saturday morning dawned crisp and sunny. Bram had nudged Zachary awake after a few hours on the couch and encouraged him into bed. He'd been about to turn and leave when Zachary's hand had reached out of the nest of blankets and grabbed his fingers, tugging him into bed.

"Stay?" Zachary had asked, and Bram's heart had soared.

Now, Zachary was still deeply asleep, but when Bram got out of bed he shifted and opened his eyes.

"I'm going to go feed Hem and take her on her walk. You keep sleeping."

Zachary nodded and buried his face back in the pillow.

Bram gave his tousled head a kiss, and left smiling.

Hemlock was waiting for him at the door with her leash on the floor next to her.

"You ready, sweetheart? Good girl."

He pulled on a sweater and clipped on her leash and they ventured out into the sunlight.

The decorations of Casper Road were starting to appear on most houses and Bram checked them out as they walked.

"Hey, Hem. I really, really like Zachary," he confided.

She yipped in response and he took that as approval.

"What if he leaves?" Bram asked.

Hemlock looked up at him, responding to the tone of his voice. She licked his hand and placed her head under it so he could scratch her ears.

He took that to mean that she'd still be there for him even if Zachary left.

"Thanks, Hem."

The leaves glowed like fire in the bright early morning sun, and there was woodsmoke on the air. It was one of Bram's favorite smells and always reminded him of Olympia and the firepit in his family's backyard. In the autumn his parents would put a pot of chili to simmer over the fire and send the kids outside to eat an early dinner around it as the sun set. At the time, it had been an adventure—so much fun to feel independent out of doors with his siblings. As an adult he realized it was so that his parents could have some peace and quiet inside while they ate together at the end of a busy day.

Smiling at the thought, he took a selfie with Casper Road laid out behind him and texted it to his parents with a note: Miss you!

He knew they wouldn't be up yet, but he liked that they'd wake up to it.

When they neared the end of the street, Bram admired Mrs. Lundy's yard of stone and stick piles, marveling as he always did at how haunting they were—even more so now with leaves caught, skeletal, in their crevices.

He thought of ringing the doorbell to say hello, but it was so early. He sent her a text too: Good morning. Just walking by and admiring your sculptures. See you on Tuesday!

Bram enjoyed their Tuesday-morning tea so much. He loved hearing stories about her life and the people she'd known. About the ways Garnet Run had changed—which were really about the way the world had changed. She seemed to enjoy hearing about his life too.

The text came immediately: Psh, son, I'm an old lady. I'm always up. Come on in if you like.

Bram grinned.

"Want to go chat with Mrs. Lundy for a minute, Hem?"

Hem cocked her head and Bram took that as a yes.

"Morning," Bram called as he let himself in.

She was in the kitchen and held out a cup of tea as he came in.

"Sit," she said.

He sat.

"Good. Now, *what* is going on with you and the Glass boy? I must have an update."

Bram laughed.

"How do you know anything's going on?" he couldn't resist teasing.

She gave him a withering look over the top of her glasses.

"I'm old, not oblivious. Not yet, anyway."

Bram sighed. In truth, he was desperate to wax poetic about Zachary, but he wasn't sure Zachary would want him talking to the neighbor about him. He could be so private.

"Go on, go on, it's obvious, and I am the soul of discretion."

She winked, but Bram didn't doubt it.

"I like him. So much. He's just…delightful."

Bram couldn't think of a better word to describe the quirky, funny, brilliant man. Zachary delighted him.

"We haven't seriously discussed it, but I could see a real future with him. I know we seem really different, but it just works?"

Mrs. Lundy cocked her head, looking so much like Hem for a moment that Bram almost laughed.

"You're both passionate, deeply feeling people. You both value honesty and fairness. And you're both clearly smitten. Ah, young love!" she opined dramatically with a sly wink.

"You can tell all that from meeting him once?" Bram asked.

"Sure. But it's also in everything you've said about him. And believe me, I know more about Zachary Glass than he might think. You forget I've been here a long time."

"So you've seen him around here, you mean?"

"Yes. But I remember when that girl went missing in Cheyenne and the Glasses moved to Garnet Run. Terrible thing. That poor family."

"I didn't realize it was such a public case," Bram said, feeling instantly foolish for not thinking to google it.

"Oh, yes. One of the largest searches in Wyoming history. And the mother—well. We all grieve in different ways."

"Yeah, she sounds like she's made her whole life about what happened, from what Zachary's told me."

Mrs. Lundy nodded.

"She spoke to every journalist and newscaster she could. And there, in the background, was her son. He was always there but she never mentioned him. It was like she had one child, and that child was gone. I would see him at Peach's sometimes, alone. Always alone. Drawing or just staring out the window. Never any friends, never with his parents. I thought he'd leave the second he finished school, like so many of the artistic ones do. But he stayed. I remember being surprised by that."

Her gaze got distant, and Bram could tell she was back in that time, seeing Zachary as he was. Bram wished he could be there. He wished that he could've known Zachary then.

"I would've been his friend," Bram said.

She cupped his cheek. "I know you would have, dear."

"He might leave now, anyway," Bram said bitterly. "He has the chance for a promotion in Denver."

Mrs. Lundy narrowed her eyes. "Well, I guess you better go with him, then. Or give him a damn good reason to stay."

When Bram got home from Mrs. Lundy's, Zachary was standing on his porch.

"Oh, hey, there you are. Hi."

"Hi," Bram said. "I was just talking to Mrs. Lundy about you."

"Oh yeah?"

"Yup. She thinks you are a passionate person who values honesty."

"Oh. Well. That's true. Hi, Hemlock."

Hem yipped, but had learned that Zachary did not appreciate being licked in greeting.

"I was just going to come find you," Bram said. "I have a proposal."

Zachary raised his eyebrows. "This is so sudden, but yes. I'd like a spring wedding."

Bram laughed. "Liar. You'd want a horror movie wedding."

"You can't have a horror movie wedding in the spring?"

Bram grinned. "You're right. Anyway, you wanna hear this or not?"

"Hear it."

They sat on the stoop in a patch of sun, warm despite the chill in the air.

"Okay, so. I think we should collaborate."

"On what?"

"On our Halloween decorations."

At the horrified look on Zachary's face, Bram clarified his thoughts.

"Wait, wait. I know you have the whole ghost ship concept that you've been working on for, like, seventy months, and I don't mean you need to change your whole plan. But I could help you execute it! And you could help me theme mine to be in conversation with yours. It would be so cool! And we could have way more impact with two yards than one."

Zachary seemed to contemplate this.

"It's true that our impact would be exponentially greater," he allowed.

Bram grinned. "Plus, it'll be fun." He bumped Zachary's shoulder with his own.

"Well, it's fun doing it on my own."

"Fun-*er*, then," Bram said, and kissed him before he could say that funner wasn't a word.

"Hmm," Zachary said. Bram kissed him again. "We can try," Zachary said. "But I would need your clear consent that I am in charge of this vision."

"I totally understand that you are in charge, oh visionary one."

Zachary narrowed his eyes but nodded, and Bram knew he'd been taken at his word.

"Yay! This is going to be so awesome," Bram declared to all of Casper Road.

Chapter Twenty

Zachary

The truth? It *was* more fun to work on the decorations with Bram than it was to do it by himself.

Once Bram had proven that he was indeed willing to honor Zachary's vision and planning, they had a blast fine-tuning some of the modes of execution of Zachary's decorations and building Bram's skills and yard into them. They even planned a concept for the street between their houses to be implemented on the day of, when the road would be closed to all but foot traffic.

Zachary's concept was of a sunken ghost ship crewed by skeletal creatures that did not resemble humans. His house would be the ship, and the creatures would be constructed out of a combination of human and animal bones (fake, of course, because he hadn't been able to source real ones). He'd been sketching the creatures for months. When in situ, they'd be lit eerily by his secret weapon—the bioluminescent algae that Wes used as the basis for his research—so that they seemed to glow with a dappled, deep-sea light. It was times like these when it paid to have a best friend who was an inventor.

The tree in Zachary's yard would become the main mast of the broken ship, with one of the creatures lashed to it, Odyssean and screaming. Other creatures would be laid throughout the lawn, clawing their way hither and yon, as if the ground were the ocean.

He'd been given strict instructions the first year, after several children were so terrified of his concept (a hospital in which a doctor had gone murderous and begun dismembering her patients) that they refused to even walk past it—*or* to go to the doctor, according to several neighbors. Now he was careful to make the concept far removed from everyday life, and the figures indistinct enough that children weren't too terrified.

When he told Bram about that injunction, Bram had breathed a sigh of relief and said, "Phew. I don't want to be too scared to approach your house."

And he'd raised his eyebrow just a little in a way that had made Zachary remember all the things they did behind closed doors. They'd exchanged heated glances over the next hour before they clasped hands and retreated behind those closed doors to do some of what they were thinking about.

They emerged, flushed and satisfied, and Bram had the idea that his chainsaw carving of the dragon could, with a little editing, become a sea monster. That led them to imagine all the ways Bram's decorations could also be made to look like they were underwater. A number of blue tarps borrowed from Charlie Matheson's woodshed made quite a compelling ocean, when anchored in waves to the ground.

The hardest part was going to be putting up the exterior of the ghost ship around his house—it was both a large job and something that had to be done last minute, since a Wyoming autumn could turn into winter faster than you could say *global climate change*.

Now, then, Zachary focused on the skeleton creatures while Bram repainted the dragon to look like a sea monster.

Several neighbors happened by. They didn't ask Zachary about his concept, knowing from past experience that he wouldn't answer.

Bram, however, was more than happy to chat about it with them all day long.

To be fair, Zachary hadn't told him that he never divulged the plan. Plus, of course, Bram was the friendliest, nicest person ever.

"This is such a great way to build community," Bram said, grinning, as he flung his arm over Zachary's shoulders after the last neighbor left. "Wanna come in?"

Zachary nodded and they went inside, Hemlock at their heels.

Bram moved around the kitchen, giving Hemlock her dinner, washing up, making them tea. They sat at the kitchen table to drink it.

"You're thinking hard about something," Bram said. "How to waterproof the ship hull?"

Zachary shook his head. Well, he *had* been thinking about that, but.

"This is fun," he said.

Bram nodded and grinned.

"But. *Fun.* I..."

"Did you not think it was gonna be fun?"

"No, it's always fun. It's always fun to plan and do the decorations. But this is..."

"Funner?" Bram teased.

"Well, yeah."

But it wasn't quite what he meant. They'd already established that it could be more fun to do something with someone else. He'd accepted it, even if he didn't like to acknowledge it. But...

"It's usually more fun to work toward a goal with someone than try to beat them at it," Bram said gently.

But historically that had not been true for Zachary. He'd always enjoyed competition. He loved being the best—loved the rush that came from realizing you were on top of the game. From knowing definitively that you won.

But, looking at Bram—generous mouth soft and tender, blue eyes always lit with some mysterious inner light, strong hand on Zachary's knee—Zachary had no desire to beat him. No desire to compete. Because competition was separation, and he wanted to be *connected* to Bram.

He'd never thought of it that way before, and it settled over him like a shroud.

When had it begun? When had he started to nourish the isolating separation of competition?

Had he been the one to do it?

He remembered being six, seven, eight, and disagreeing with kids on the playground. They agreed with each other and in his separateness he wanted to be right. Being right, being *best*, was the consolation for being alone.

Maybe it didn't matter why or how he learned it.

By high school it was no longer consolation, but vocation. His classmates tormented him—why on earth would he want to be connected to them? All he wanted was to grind them to dust and maintain some semblance of self.

Plus…he liked being right. He liked being smart. He'd never been attractive or funny, never been likable or popular. There were only so many things you could be.

Right?

Bram was watching him closely. Zachary felt like one of those deep-sea creatures that lived only in the dark—the kind so translucent you could see their organs through their bodies. He felt like Bram was looking all the way inside him and watching his thoughts as they happened.

It was unnerving and made him squirmy. He thought maybe this superpower was what people called empathy.

He closed his eyes to escape it.

Bram kissed his cheek, then poured them more tea.

"Hey, my family is going to play Pictionary. Wanna play?"

Somehow Zachary found himself nodding and then they were video calling into a room full of people who all erupted into an enthusiastic welcome when Bram appeared on their screen.

Had Bram always had this? This entire group of people happy simply to be in his presence?

"Hi, Zachary!" some of them were saying.

"Oh. Hey. Hello. Hi." He waved.

The game was familiar, but the Larkspurs played by their own rules and had so many previous games in their collective family knowledge that half of the guesses seemed to be references to previous things they had drawn.

When Moon drew an umbrella and Trent guessed "a baby," they all dissolved into laughter.

"Be back," Zachary murmured, and went to the bathroom.

In the mirror, his eyes looked wild and his expression suspicious. He didn't know how to be with these people. They were so close that even their competition was actually togetherness. They just wanted to have fun together.

Zachary remembered when he was thirteen and Sarah was sixteen and she would call him into her room. He would read while she stared out the window, listening to music on her headphones. When he asked her why she wanted them to do two separate things in the same room, she'd said, "I like coexisting with you."

She was, he was pretty sure, the only person who ever had.

Zachary had been thinking about her a lot recently. He wasn't sure if it was the call from his mom or telling the story to Bram. Both. Neither. But he'd been remembering more of the before, lately. More of what he'd lost when he'd lost her.

His mother acted like she was the only one who had lost. His father had gone away somewhere inside his head and Zachary didn't know what it was like in there. If it contained his sister or not. But seeing Bram's family, he realized something he'd never considered before.

His mother had never asked him if he knew anything about her disappearance. The police had. Strangers had. But his mother hadn't even considered that he might know anything. She'd never considered that Sarah might confide in him or that he might have insight into her actions.

She hadn't ever told him how sorry she was that he had lost his sister. She hadn't really realized they were close.

"Are you okay, baby?"

Bram, come to check on him.

Zachary opened the door and Bram's expression was instantly worried.

"What's wrong?" He pulled Zachary into his arms. "Is my family too much? I know they're a lot. We can hang up if you want?"

Zachary shook his head.

"I don't want to hang up. I was just thinking."

"Oh yeah? About what?"

Laughter and indistinct chatter floated in from the other room. Bram was totally focused on him.

"About togetherness."

Chapter Twenty-One

Bram

Bram fell in love with Zachary Glass standing in a bathroom.

He didn't ask what Zachary meant when he said he was thinking of togetherness, because he already knew. He didn't think he'd ever seen a clearer expression of longing than he'd seen on Zachary's face, the laughter of the Larkspurs a distant soundtrack to his desire. So Bram just pulled Zachary to him and cupped the back of his neck. He didn't say *I love you*, but when he said "*I've got you,*" it was what he meant. And Zachary had sighed and pushed closer against him as if it was all he'd wanted to hear.

That night, after finishing the chaotic and rousing game of Pictionary with his family, Zachary fell asleep in Bram's arms and had nightmares all night. He woke up gasping and reached for Bram. Bram held him as he shuddered and fell back asleep.

Zachary didn't offer up the contents of the dreams, but in his sleep he pushed at something or someone. He mumbled, "Leave me alone." He pulled the covers over his head.

Bram wasn't foolish enough to think that pain was the same thing as depth, but goddamn if Zachary didn't have layers, and Bram wanted to learn every one of them.

Not slough them off, or peel them away, but honor them—every one of them—because they were all part of the man he loved.

"It's too soon," he said to Hemlock on a long walk the next morning, after Zachary had gone to work and the morning rain had given way to glorious autumn sun. "But he's so…lovely."

Maybe *lovely* wasn't a word that most people would use to describe Zachary, but Bram knew it was the right one.

Hem yipped in agreement, so there was that.

Was it too soon? You couldn't control how fast you fell for someone, could you? Maybe not. But you could try and control whether you made the same mistakes again and again. Mistakes like slotting someone into a future you were creating for yourself instead of actually falling for *them*.

But with Zachary he knew he wasn't repeating what had happened with Drake. Mostly because it was *hard* to slot Zachary into any kind of future he'd imagined for himself. Zachary wasn't very slottable. No,

Bram had no doubt that his feelings were for Zachary himself.

What he was really trying to figure out was whether it was too soon to tell Zachary he'd fallen for him.

In that moment, Bram pulled out his phone to call Naveen, forgetting that Naveen wasn't his best friend anymore. He winced as the pain rushed in.

He and Hem turned off the path and hiked up a rocky hillside to another path through the woods.

"I got my heart crushed, but that's *not* a reason to never love someone again," Bram was explaining to Hemlock.

They walked in silence for a while, Bram breathing deep of the fresh, piney air. Then they turned onto a small path that cut into the trees and up ahead, something very strange appeared.

"Is something...glowing?" Bram asked.

Hemlock tugged at her leash, pulling him toward it.

The path opened up to a small clearing and in it, trees glowed like something from another world.

"Oh my god," Bram breathed. They were beautiful and strange, giving off a dim but luminous brilliance, and seemed somehow like a sign from the universe that he was right to love the beautiful, strange, luminous, and brilliant Zachary Glass.

He couldn't wait to tell Zachary about what he'd seen.

Bram was making dinner when Zachary knocked on his door. He knew it was Zachary because Zachary always knocked exactly twice.

"Hey, baby!" He kissed him and drew him inside. "How was your day?"

Zachary's eyes were bright, and he was grinning. "I got the promotion."

Bram's heart sank as pride in Zachary bloomed.

"Congratulations!" He made himself say that before he said anything else. "How will it change your daily life?"

"I'll be in a more supervisory role, working with other architects to assign projects and approve them. So it'll all be very structured and orderly." That clearly pleased him. "I'll actually be doing less design, but that's expected given my supervisory capacity. It's more money. Although the cost of living in Denver is much higher than here, so it probably evens out."

His eyes went faraway, like he was doing math in his head.

Bram had tried very hard to express his positive feelings first, but when Zachary uttered the word *Denver*, Bram's whole world skidded to a stop and he sank down into the easy chair he'd recently bought.

"So you're…you're leaving, then? For sure?"

He thought he was probably going to cry. A lot.

Again. He was being left by the man he loved *again*. Maybe he hadn't told Zachary he loved him. Maybe the circumstances were different. But Bram's heart didn't care about fairness or circumstance. All it felt was devastation.

"I don't suppose you'd, um. Would you want to move to Denver?" Zachary asked.

It was so clearly an afterthought—apparently he hadn't given even one second's contemplation to the fact that moving would separate them—that Bram goggled at him.

"Well, I just mean, um. You moved all the way here from Washington, so it wouldn't be a big deal maybe."

He bit his lip.

Bram stood up and started pacing.

"I moved here because I was a total wreck. I sold everything I owned and came here because I needed someplace that was just mine. That didn't make me think of betrayal and heartbreak everywhere I looked. Because this place felt good to me. Fresh and clean and—and nature. I don't want to live in some dirty city."

He could hear the panic and pain in his voice, but Zachary just frowned.

"Actually, Denver was just rated as being the second-best city to live in in the United—"

Bram threw up his hands. He realized, with an absent, this-indicates-growth thought, that he should not have kept his feelings about this bottled up for the last few days in an attempt to be chill. He should've sat Zachary down and told him exactly how he felt. But he hadn't and now it was too late.

"That's not what I meant! I can't believe we're... and you're gonna just *leave*!"

"Well, I..." Zachary began. He looked confused and uncertain. "I...didn't think it would matter," Zachary said.

"Wouldn't *matter*? How's that?"

"I thought... I assumed you'd be gone by the time it happened," Zachary said resignedly.

His tone was mild, but the words landed like a spear through Bram's heart. He'd felt like the edges of his new life were being folded up as neatly and elegantly as origami. But no. It had been crumpled up like one of Zachary's rejected sketches.

"I need you to give me some space right now," Bram choked out. The tears were about to come, and Bram didn't want Zachary to see.

"I don't... I... Are you mad at me?" Zachary asked. He sounded forlorn and he looked so small.

"Yeah," Bram said. "Yeah, I'm mad and I'm really sad and I gotta cry in private now. Can you take off, please?"

Zachary slipped out of the house like a ghost and closed the door quietly behind him.

Bram swore, then his words were lost to crying. Hem, sweet Hem, stuck her nose in his face where he'd sat down on the floor and licked the tears from his cheeks. She dropped her chin onto his knee, her warmth the only thing keeping him grounded. He wrapped his arms around her and let out a shaky breath.

If he'd thought that going through two heartbreaks already this year might've tempered the pain of this one, he'd been very wrong.

This pain wasn't betrayal. Zachary hadn't really done anything wrong. This pain was pure and clean.

Bram had fallen in love with Zachary Glass and now Zachary Glass was leaving.

Chapter Twenty-Two

Zachary

Zachary was mostly numb with a kind of itch in his brain. The itch usually meant that he was missing something—some bit of information or connection required to understand something that other people seemed to understand intuitively.

Bram was sad he was leaving. That made sense. Bram was mad Zachary hadn't told him sooner. That made sense. He could see that he could've been clearer.

But none of that accounted for Bram's…he could only call it devastation.

He hated to see Bram like that. Bram, who was usually sunshine and smiles and excited energy.

He'd thought Bram would be proud of him. When he'd gotten the call, Fisk had said, "Congratulations,

Glass. You're going to do wonderfully," and Zachary had looked in the mirror and felt pure pride. He was the youngest-ever junior partner in Moray and Fisk history. He had won. By every metric, he'd won.

Now when he looked in the mirror, he just felt confused and sad. So shockingly, distractingly sad. He couldn't do anything like this. Couldn't stand to feel like this when he didn't understand why.

Up until a few months ago, Zachary's best friend Wes had conducted their whole relationship over the phone or via video chats because he didn't like to leave the house or have people in his space. All of which had suited Zachary just fine.

Recently, though, after falling in love with Adam and coparenting his daughter, Gus, Wes consented to the occasional outing and didn't mind visitors.

So when Zachary knocked on his door and no one answered, he went to Adam's house right across the street.

Huh. Just like Bram and me, he thought.

But of course, it *wasn't* just like him and Bram because Wes and Adam were in love and raising a kid together and Zachary and Bram were just…

Anyway.

Adam answered the door and smiled. "Hey, Zachary! Wes, Zachary's here," he called, waving Zachary inside.

Wes and Gus came into the room, hands covered in something brightly colored and unidentifiable.

"Hey, Zachary," Wes said. "We were working on Gus' science project."

Zachary nodded. "Got a minute, Wes?"

"Sure. You can do the next part on your own, right, Gus?"

"I don't want to," she said.

"Honey," Adam said, "remember we talked about how sometimes things come up and we need to be flexible?"

Gus nodded.

"Well, Zachary needs Wes right now."

"But I don't feel like being flexible right now," Gus said.

Zachary really related.

Adam laughed. "Go do your work, Bug."

"Fine," Gus sighed. "I hope this is important, Zachary."

She said it sincerely and he responded in kind.

"It is."

They nodded at one another and Gus trudged out of the room.

"What's up?" Wes asked.

Wes sat him down at the kitchen table, and Adam offered him some pie.

"I just made it. I'm learning to bake," Adam said, turning to the pie.

Wes caught his eye and gave a subtle shake of his head, but Zachary did want some pie.

"Thanks," he said when Adam set the plate in front of him.

He took a bite. It was cherry. At least, it looked like cherry. But it tasted like…

"Hmm. Something has gone very wrong with the chemistry of your baking," Zachary explained, and pushed the plate away.

"Oh. Shoot," Adam said, frowning. He took a small

bite of the pie from Zachary's plate. And screwed up his face.

"Gah, what did I *do*? I swear, I follow the instructions, but that's... Sorry, Zachary."

"That's okay."

"You look like hell," Wes said. "What's up?"

"I got the promotion."

"Oh, wow. Congrats," Wes said.

"Congratulations!" Adam said.

"Thanks. It means I'm the youngest-ever junior partner in the company," Zachary said, waiting for them to be impressed.

"Great," Wes said anemically.

"That sounds very prestigious," Adam said.

"Yes," Zachary confirmed.

This wasn't how it was supposed to go. Wes and Adam were supposed to be impressed. They were supposed to realize that he was talented and impressive.

But they were just nodding mildly.

"Anyway, it's an accomplishment, but when I told Bram about it he was really mad at me for leaving."

"Leaving?" Adam said.

"Yes, well, of course, the company is headquartered in Denver, so that's where a junior partner needs to be."

What about this were people not getting?

"Oh, damn," Wes said, looking shocked. "I didn't know you'd be leaving. That's so...wow."

Zachary wasn't sure why it would matter to Wes, given that the entirety of their relationship before six months ago had taken place remotely anyway, but he looked genuinely disappointed.

"Yes, of course."

Adam looked at him kindly. "I think since you work from home, no one knew that a promotion would change that."

Wes nodded.

"Well, be that as it may, Bram is mad at me and..."

Sad. He'd said sad.

"And sad, and he told me to go away, and I don't know how to fix it."

"What exactly did he say?" Wes asked.

"He said he didn't want to move to a dirty city. Then that he was mad and sad and he needed to cry privately so could I please leave."

Adam bit his lip. "You asked him to move with you?"

"Yeah. I assumed we'd be over by now since people always lose interest in me, but somehow he hasn't yet, so."

Zachary heard his voice go gritty and thin. The scene before him blurred.

"I wanted him to be proud of me. I wanted him to be impressed," Zachary said. "But he was just mad."

And sad. Don't forget sad. Don't forget you dimmed the sun.

"Hard to care about career success when your boyfriend is leaving you, Z," Wes said.

"Did I screw up?" Zachary heard himself ask. The scene was blurring more, and Adam reached over and brushed something off his cheek.

"Maybe. You really like Bram or are you just glad he hasn't lost interest?"

Zachary pictured Bram's happy blue eyes, the way he smiled at people and meant it, how much he loved his family, the single-minded attention he paid to the *swick* of his knife through wood or to a kiss. He thought of the way they fell over each other laughing when Mr. Purcell saw the Christmas lights on his lawn and how Bram reached for his hand when he got scared. He thought of the warm comfort that sank into his very bones when he and Bram lay tangled in bed together.

"I really, really, *really* like him."

Wes nodded somberly. "Have you told him that?"

Zachary blinked. "I…don't know. No."

"Step one is tell him how you feel about him."

"But," Adam interjected, "if you know you're going to take this promotion and move, and you know he doesn't want to go… Just, don't give him hope that you might stay if you know you aren't."

"*If* I take it?"

Of course he was taking it. He was the *youngest junior partner ever!* How, oh *how*, were people not getting this?

"Well, yeah," Wes said. "You've been really frustrated for a while now that you don't get to do as many projects on your own terms. Will that change now?"

"This will be more of a supervisory role. More mentoring other people and reviewing their work."

"But you hate other people."

Adam snorted.

"I like telling them what to do," Zachary clarified. "This is a stepping stone. Junior partner means partner someday. And once I'm partner…"

Adam and Wes were both watching him expectantly.

"Well, then I'll be in charge."

"But...will you get to do more of your own designs?" Wes asked again.

"No, I just told you." Zachary was getting exasperated.

Adam put a hand on Wes' arm, but Wes was looking at Zachary.

"Z. This promotion is very impressive."

Finally! That was what he had been wanting to hear!

So why didn't Wes sound happy for him?

"But it also sounds like it will mean doing *less* of the part of your job that you value, and doing *more* of the things that you have never enjoyed. It would also mean moving to Colorado, which you've never mentioned wanting to do. In fact, you worked hard to convince the firm to let you work remotely so you could stay in Garnet Run. So, even though it's an impressive vote of confidence in your abilities, it sounds like... well, like it would suck for you."

Zachary's head was spinning. The perfectly ordered plan that had previously been color-coded in his mind was swirling, the colors mixing to a muddy and unsatisfying brown.

"But...but I got the promotion," Zachary murmured, but it didn't seem as uncomplicatedly positive as it had before.

Chapter Twenty-Three

Bram

He'd cried. Then he'd gotten on his motorcycle, driven into the skin-chafing wind, and let its punishing whip dry his tears. Then he'd pulled over and cried some more.

His feelings for Zachary had snuck up on him. Snaked their way inside like delicate roots that thickened and became a tree—slow, thriving, ineluctable.

Back home, he curled up in bed with a nest of blankets, patted the bed for Hem, and pulled her close.

Although he was closest with Moon, there was one person he called when he truly didn't know what to do.

"Dad?" he croaked. "I'm… I'm all messed up again."

"Oh, my Bramble. Tell me."

He heard his dad murmur something and then the sounds of the door shutting behind him.

He could picture it exactly. His dad had said "It's Bram," to his mom, in the voice that meant, *I'll go take care of this*, and then walked outside, probably to sit on the stump next to the pumpkin bed.

Bram told his father what had happened. The promotion. The move. The clumsy request that Bram drop everything and tag along behind him like a stuffed animal that would be left in an airport or a diner in a moment of carelessness or outgrowth.

"If he'd asked you differently would you want to go?" his dad asked.

Bram hadn't thought about it. "I don't know. I like it here, but..."

"But Zachary is a big part of what you like."

What would Casper Road be like without its resident Zachary Glass?

"Yeah."

But that wasn't even the point.

"I thought I could trust him," Bram said. "Why do I keep falling for people who I can't trust?"

Hem responded to his distress by pawing at him and sticking her nose in his neck. He cuddled her closer. At least she would never let him down.

"Oh, son. I know you're hurting. You've always expected so much of people. It makes it even worse when they disappoint you."

He thought his boyfriend and his best friend having an affair behind his back was a little more than *disappointing*, but his dad went on.

"But trust isn't something that lives in other people. It is a choice that you make for yourself. And it's a choice you have to make over and over."

The wind whistled on his dad's end and Bram could

picture him walking among the raised beds at the tree line, knew that it would smell like fresh moss and decomposing leaves and woodsmoke.

He was stricken suddenly with a pang of longing so sharp he nearly gasped.

"Trust is showing up and being vulnerable and honest with another person. It's choosing to believe they have good or reasonable intentions. It's standing up for yourself, so you teach them how to treat you. And all of that—all of it—comes from you."

Bram closed his eyes and listened hard.

"My biggest worry for you," his father went on, "has always been that you don't trust *yourself.* You look to others for something that can only come from within. The most important trust is that you are enough as you are and always will be, no matter who you have or don't have in your life."

A tear slid down Bram's cheek.

"You don't need your siblings to tell you what you should do. You don't need me, either. You need to look inside yourself and see what Bram wants. What Bram needs. Learn to trust yourself, or no demonstration of trustworthiness in anyone else will matter."

Later, after hanging up with his dad, Bram pulled the covers over his head and let himself drift inside his cocoon. Let himself drift in the ether of Bram-ness and all that it entailed.

What did he want? What did he need? Why was it so hard for him to not call his siblings and see if he was right?

The two knocks that meant Zachary sounded on the door, pulling Bram out of a fitful sleep.

He lay there for a moment, deciding whether or not he wanted to see Zachary. It had been four long days of nesting in his bed, reading old X-Men comics, and leaving the house only to take Hem out. It turned out that breaking up with someone who lived right across the street was hell on your mobility.

The Zachary Glass he opened the door to was a shadow. Already slim, he looked like he'd lost weight, his usually olive complexion was sallow, and he had dark circles under his eyes. His hair looked dirty. But his eyes were wild and awake.

When he spoke it came out in a rush.

"I know you're mad and sad at me and I know you asked for space, but I really need my friend right now. Is there any way you could forget that we were… whatever and just be my friend for a minute? If you say no, I promise I'll leave, and I'm sorry if I'm butting in, but I just… I really need to talk to my best friend right now," he concluded, with a break in his voice.

Best friend. He'd missed having one these last few months. It tore at Bram's defenses and he opened the door, too curious and ever hopeful for the self-preservation of distance.

"Okay," he said.

"Thank you," Zachary sighed. He settled on the bench at the kitchen table and Bram made tea automatically.

"So, there's this guy," Zachary began. "And I really, really like him. At first we were just friends, but then things got, um, romantic? And I have the best time with him. I kept expecting that he'd get sick of me or annoyed, because everyone else seems to. And then they leave. But he didn't. And now I got this promotion, but it would mean moving away from him. At first I was definitely going to take it. Because getting promoted is a good thing. But now…now I don't know. Wes pointed out that the part I like most about my current job is the part I won't get to do anymore in my new position. And that even now I don't get to do it the *way* I want. But maybe later, after I'm junior partner and then full partner, when I'm in charge even more, I'll probably get to do more of what I want. I think. I guess I'm not sure."

He was looking very intently at his own hands.

"So now I don't know what to do. I never meant to hurt the guy I like. I even asked him to maybe come with me, but I think I did it wrong. And I could just really, really use your help untangling it." After a beat, he said, "The end."

Bram blew out a breath and set the mugs of tea down in front of them.

"Well," he said, keeping his voice even. "It sounds like you had something really great going with this guy. Sounds like he really likes you and maybe he was just nervous about that because he's been burned before. It also sounds like you have two realities going on. Reality number one is that you love designing your unique creative buildings, and this promotion will *not* let you do that and *will* force you to do work you hate. In that reality, the answer is clear. Don't take the promotion."

Zachary frowned and opened his mouth, but Bram went on.

"In reality number two, you clearly value external approval like promotions and praise. And in that reality, just *getting* the promotion is a reward in and of itself."

Zachary shut his mouth, brown furrowed.

"As your friend, here's what I would say. Whether or not you take the promotion, you still *got* it. You got the acclaim and approval. Turning it down doesn't take that away. But the thing about external approval is that it doesn't do anything for the day-by-day living of your life. Like, knowing you achieved a promotion doesn't help you out if for the next ten years you hate having it. *You're* the one who needs to approve of yourself."

Pieces clicked into place and Bram realized that this was precisely what his father had been trying to tell him.

"Can I ask you a question?" Zachary nodded. "How do you feel when you design something, and you *know* it's really good?"

A slow smile crept across Zachary's mouth. "Proud of myself. Triumphant. Satisfied."

"You don't need anyone to tell you those designs are good because you know it."

"Yeah."

"I've been realizing lately," Bram said slowly, "that mostly we need approval and esteem about the things we're not confident about. I don't need to know what anyone thinks about how I walk the dog, because I know I do it just fine. But I do ask for other people to advise me about my relationships because I worry I don't do them right. Do you know why you need so much external approval?"

He asked it gently, and then fell silent, sipping the chamomile tea and waiting for Zachary to answer.

Zachary's brow furrowed and he frowned into his

tea like he could menace the answer forth from the depths of his cup.

"I was never someone that people liked," he said. It wasn't a bid for disagreement, just a fact as Zachary saw it, so Bram stayed silent. "I was always different and whatever I did seemed to announce that to everyone. It made it…easy, I guess, for people to cut me down. Children don't have a shred of mercy in them. At least they didn't for me. Every day, all day, I was different and wrong and weird and…" He shook his head. "It went on until Sarah disappeared. Then they were all too awkward to mess with me because now I was more pathetic than they could ever tease me for. In a way…" He chewed his lip. "In a way, her disappearance was the best thing that ever happened to me."

Bram could tell that the guilt over this reality weighed heavily on Zachary.

"I was never the one anyone liked. Never the one anyone rooted for. But I was smart. And when teachers praised me it felt good." He shrugged. "It was the other students I wanted to think I was smart or cool or attractive, but they didn't, so at least I could get the highest grade or finish the test first. It was…there was no space for me in any of those other competitions, but in this one, I could win."

Bram's heart broke at the thought of young Zachary desperately wanting the love and approval of his classmates and being denied it at every turn. No wonder he needed people to know he was successful, that he was valued.

He looked up finally and met Bram's eyes. "I couldn't believe you liked me."

"I did," Bram said definitively.

Zachary's eyelashes fluttered and he swallowed. "Past tense?"

"I do," Bram clarified. "I do like you, Zachary. Don't ever doubt that."

A tear landed in Zachary's tea and he drank it down, draining his cup.

"Okay," Bram said. "Here's what I think—as your friend. I think your firm sucks."

Zachary's chin jerked up.

"I know, I know, they're the most prestigious firm in the Middle West. Whatever that means. But who *cares* about their prestige if they don't value the work that is unique to you?"

Again, Zachary opened his mouth, but Bram was on a roll.

"They don't, Zachary! They value your *skill*, because it means you're never the squeaky wheel. They value your work ethic, because you probably get more done in a day than most people do in a week. They value your loyalty to the company, because that means you'll put up with anything. But none of that is the same thing. They don't like the work that is the most *you*. That *you* like the best. So, as your friend, I am telling you. Don't take their promotion. And don't settle for a firm that only wants your rote ability, not the creative genius that makes you you."

Zachary's eyes were wide. "Quit? You think I should quit my job?"

"Hell yeah! Find a firm that *loves* your weird horror alien designs."

"They're not alien—"

"Find a firm that *values* Zachary Glass. Or go freelance. Just don't waste one more brilliant design on people who make you shave off everything about it that makes it unique. Don't spend your life designing boxes when you could be doing so much more."

He hadn't even realized how impassioned he was coming across until he was standing up and concluding with a booming voice.

And as his words rang out in the silence of the house he'd just begun to think of as home, Bram Larkspur realized that he was addressing himself just as much as he was Zachary.

"Wow," Zachary murmured. "Does that advice apply to other areas of my life too?"

"Hmm?" Bram asked, but he was distracted because Zachary was rounding the table and coming to stand right in front of him.

"Because did I mention there's this guy...?"

Bram was exhausted and hungry and dirty, and his hair was sticking up on one side from the pillows in his nest, but all he wanted in the entire world was to kiss Zachary Glass.

"I think my breath is bad," Bram said.

"I don't care."

"I kinda haven't showered in a few days on account of being in a blanket nest."

"I don't care."

"I'm all—"

"Shut up unless you don't want me to kiss you."

Bram shut his mouth on a comically loud "meep."

Zachary put his hands on Bram's shoulders. "I'm so sorry I went about telling you about the promotion all wrong," he murmured. "And I'm sorry I didn't tell you more clearly how I felt."

"How do you feel?" Bram let himself murmur.

"I really, really, *really* like you," he said, eyes intent on Bram's mouth.

"I would like to take those three *really*s and trade them in for a hotel," Bram said.

Zachary stopped. "Uh. What?"

"I was…um, sorry. Monopoly reference. Well, we didn't play Monopoly as kids; we had this noncapitalist version where you worked together to distribute wealth, but the point is when you get three houses in Monopoly you could trade them in for hotels and you said you really, really, really, and I. Or was it four houses? Hmm. Anyway, please kiss me and put us both out of my misery now."

Zachary smiled and kissed Bram passionately.

Bram groaned, arms coming around Zachary's back to hold him close. They kissed deeply, pulling back every so often to look at each other and smile.

"I missed you so much," Bram said.

"The idea of Colorado was shit without you, anyway," Zachary said. "Also, Monopoly was invented to demonstrate that capitalistic monopolies were a *bad* thing."

"You don't say," Bram muttered, grabbing him by the hand and dragging him down the hallway.

They entered the bedroom to find Hemlock tucked into the blanket nest, looking like the pearl in an oyster. One of her ears was inside the blankets and one was sticking out. Bram grabbed his phone off the bedside table and snapped a picture. He spared a moment to press a gentle kiss to Hem's ears. His constant companion. His darling.

Then he dragged Zachary into the bathroom and started the shower.

"We need to be clean for all the things I wanna do to you," Bram muttered between kisses.

"I am clean," Zachary managed before Bram kissed him again.

The shower was quick and dirty—well, quick and clean—and Bram tried to psychically send Hemlock a message to be out of the bed when they got there.

Bram had always been pretty sure that telepathy was possible and was delighted to be proven right. He stripped the blankets off the bed and lay down on it, arms out for Zachary.

"I missed having you in my bed," he murmured, and Zachary shivered. "I missed the feel of your skin," he went on. He could see the effect his words were having, and he spared a moment of devastation that Zachary had heard so little praise that he valued it so highly, but whatever the reason, Bram was happy to give it to him.

"You taste so good," he said as they kissed. Zachary moaned. "You feel perfect in my arms." Zachary's breaths were shallow and fast, and Bram pressed him into the sheets and dropped a trail of kisses from his mouth to his throat and down over his ribs. Zachary writhed under his questing touch.

When he nuzzled between Zachary's thighs, Zachary spread for him. He kissed the soft skin, up one thigh to his groin, and down the other side. Zachary moaned.

"This okay?" he asked, flicking his tongue back between Zachary's ass cheeks.

He was answered with an even more enthusiastic moan.

He flipped Zachary over onto his stomach, parted his flesh, and traced his hole with a delicate tongue.

The more he lavished Zachary with attention, the more he moaned and writhed beneath Bram. Bram felt like a god. He speared Zachary with his slick tongue and Zachary groaned deliriously. When he couldn't take anymore, he kissed up to the small of Zachary's back, then up his spine to the nape of his neck to whisper in his ear.

"What do you want, baby?"

"You, you," Zachary chanted.

"Yeah?"

A groan and a nod. Bram got a condom and drizzled lube over his erection. He was buzzing with desire and wanted to watch Zachary come apart.

He slid inside Zachary and it felt like coming home. The slow parting of flesh was a divine welcome and Bram didn't want to ever leave.

Zachary scrabbled at the sheets and gasped, arching his back.

"Okay, baby?"

Zachary nodded and Bram gathered him close and kissed the nape of his neck, waiting. When Zachary relaxed, Bram began to move. Zachary felt like heaven around him and his every nerve ending sizzled.

"I missed this," Zachary said into the pillow. Then, turning to look back at Bram, "I missed you."

"I missed you too."

Bram couldn't get close enough to Zachary. He wrapped him up in his arms and thrust faster, searching for the angle that would make Zachary scream.

When he found it, Zachary went wild in his arms and he let the full weight of pleasure crash down around him.

Zachary came with a broken cry and it snapped

Bram's control. Pleasure spilled from him, cresting in an orgasm that roared through him like a tidal wave. He groaned into Zachary's neck, wanting it to last forever.

When they were lying together, sleepy and touch drunk, Zachary murmured, "Does your family hate me now?"

"What? No. Of course not. Why?"

"You tell them everything. I figured you told them how mad at me you were."

Bram winced. "Well. Yeah, I did. But being mad at someone doesn't mean hating them."

"I know," Zachary said, but the relief Bram could see in his face said otherwise.

"They don't hate you," Bram said, and kissed him. They fell asleep wrapped in each other's arms.

Chapter Twenty-Four

Zachary

The week since they'd reconciled had been one of the best weeks of Zachary's life.

Every evening, they'd worked on their decorations, and today they'd taken a long ride on Bram's motorcycle. As they looped back toward home, Bram said, "I want to show you something magical."

They walked into the woods and Bram told him to close his eyes and take his hand. After a few minutes (and one near miss with a low-hanging branch), Bram stilled him with hands on his shoulders and said, "Okay, open them."

They were in a clearing in the woods in which several trees and numerous plants seemed to glow.

Zachary started to laugh.

"Right?!" Bram said, grinning. "How are they glowing? I don't know but it's magical as hell!"

Zachary shook his head.

"Wes."

"Hmm?"

"Wes planted these. My friend who works with bio-luminescence."

Bram narrowed his eyes. "For real?"

Zachary realized in all the diagrams he'd drawn to show Bram the pieces they needed to build for the ghost ship, he had only described the eerie lighting, not said it would be coming from bioluminescent algae. Not wanting this to be another instance of assuming Bram knew things he hadn't told him, he decided to just show him.

Zachary directed Bram to Wes's house and texted they were on their way.

"One sec," he said as they dismounted. "How do you feel about spiders and snakes." He didn't want Bram to be scared.

"Good," Bram said.

"Okay." Zachary took his hand and led him up the stairs.

Wes opened the door and ran a hand over his shorn hair.

"Hey, guys. I hear you found my secret place," he said to Bram.

"It's amazing. When I wandered in there I seriously thought I was hallucinating. Then I thought maybe magic was real."

Something in Bram's voice gave Zachary the sense he was a bit sad to realize magic was not real.

"Cool. You wanna see some more?"

"Absolutely," Bram said.

Wes hesitated for a moment and Zachary said, "I already asked him. He's not scared."

Wes looked relieved and gestured them inside.

Though they'd been friends for years, Zachary had only been inside Wes' house a handful of times and each time there was something new going on.

"Is that a biogas generator?!" Bram exclaimed, walking up to it.

"Yeah. You know about them?"

"Oh yeah. My mom made one once to try and run our house with biogas and solar power only. It was amazing, until—"

"It exploded?" Wes guessed.

"Big-time. Unfortunately right when my brother, who was going through a phase where he was super embarrassed that we lived off the grid, brought this girl he really liked home. He was trying so hard to make her think we were a normal family, and then this bag of rotting food goo exploded all over her."

Wes winced, though it was unclear if it was for the girl or the biogas generator.

"God, my parents would *love* to hear about bioluminescent plants. Would you mind if I told them about it?"

"No, that's great. I'm trying to create sustainable alternatives to electric light, so it would be useful to talk with people who've transitioned into…"

And that was the point at which Zachary tuned out and went in search of Bettie, the tarantula, for company.

Bram and Wes were fast friends, discussing everything from sustainability to the benefits and detriments of daylight savings time, and Wes gave him a tour of his basement, where all his experiments in bioluminescence took place. Zachary found Bettie and Bram took a selfie with her sitting on his head that he gleefully sent to his family, along with the promise that he had some very exciting things to tell them about bioluminescence.

When they left, Bram extracted a promise from Wes that they'd meet up soon to discuss all this further and Wes inclined his head. He looked pleased. For someone who'd spent a lot of his life trying to avoid being seen, Zachary was glad that the tides were turning for him.

Of course, as they were leaving, Adam's daughter, Gus, came running out of the house, eyes huge, Adam on her tail, and said, "That is a motorcycle. *So cool!*"

Zachary glanced up just in time to see the look of abject fear that crossed Adam's face and said, "Motorcycles are death traps."

"What's a death trap?" Gus asked, eyes even brighter.

"Well, that backfired," Adam muttered.

"Can I go on the death trap?" Gus asked, pulling at Bram's hand.

"Sorry, buddy," he said. "You've got to be a lot bigger before you can go on a motorcycle."

She visibly drooped but brightened when Bram said, "But if you want to see something *really* cool and scary, you should come to Casper Road for Halloween on Monday night."

"Can we go, Daddy?"

"Absolutely," Adam said, and mouthed *Thank you* to Bram.

"Your friends are nice," Bram said happily, then waved at them as they sped away.

Halloween dawned crisp and clear, and Zachary sprang out of bed, ready for the final install. Today, they would complete the transformation of the exterior of his house into the hull of the ghost ship.

The pieces were stacked in a complicated system throughout the living room, and excitement about the install aside, Zachary would be thrilled to have his space back, clean and uncluttered.

Bram opened the door, calling, "Happy Halloween! I come bearing coffee."

Zachary met him at the door with a grin.

"Babe, it's the day! Are you so excited?" Bram asked, handing Zachary a mug of coffee.

Zachary nodded enthusiastically. Then, because Bram's coffee was made of mushrooms and tasted like dirt, he took it into the kitchen and dumped sugar into it.

"Okay," he said. "I've made a flow chart of the install. Let me guide you through it."

He spread the paper on the kitchen table.

"You're so freaking adorable," Bram said fondly, and came up behind him. He wrapped his arms around Zachary and kissed the side of his neck. "Okay, show me."

"Okay, so."

Zachary had put a lot of thought into the flow chart, estimating time to completion of each phase of the process, and leaving a buffer of two hours for when something inevitably went wrong.

When he finished taking Bram through it, Bram said, "You're so good at this."

"I know. I've won six years running."

Bram's smile was amused.

"Yes, I know. It's very impressive." Zachary beamed. "But I meant *this*. Planning, organizing. Estimating."

"Well, yeah. It's part of my job."

It was essential to understand how the pieces fit together in a design. If you drafted something that worked on paper but couldn't be reasonably constructed, it was useless. A folly.

"Yeah, I know. I just like to remind you that you have a ton of skills and could totally be in business for yourself."

Zachary stared at the flow chart.

Ever since he and Bram had reconciled the week before, he'd been thinking about what Bram had said. About his options. About a firm that would appreciate what he actually loved doing, not just the skills he happened to possess.

He'd even poked around a bit to see if anyone was hiring. So far, nothing, but it was a constant awareness in the back of his mind, that little voice that had previously sounded like his parents, then his teachers, later his bosses. For a moment, the voice had even sounded like Bram's. *You can do it, baby!*

But over the last few days, as he paged through all the buildings he'd designed and shelved over the previous ten years, and thought, *Holy crap, these are really good*, the voice had begun to sound, more and more, like his own.

And that voice said: *Your work is practical and in-*

novative. Which would you rather be: a junior part-
ner in a firm that designs boxes, or a renegade, like
McTeague, who creates things that are inspiring and
controversial and move design forward?

And when he put it like that to himself, the answer
was clear.

Something else, too, had been happening over the
last few days.

He'd started to dream about Sarah. It hadn't happened in years, and even then they had just been vague
impressions of their childhood spun out in dream logic.

These, though, he hadn't had since the year she disappeared. These were dreams so realistic and vivid that
he woke expecting to see her walking past his door into
the bathroom or sitting at the kitchen table. Dreams
of hanging out the way they used to—coexisting, as
she'd always said—and watching movies on opposite
sides of the couch, her jabbing a nail-bitten finger at
the screen to explicate an effect or call out a clumsy
bit of foreshadowing.

The thing that he had never told anyone—not the
police and not his parents—was that he hadn't been
surprised when one day she was gone. He'd been
shocked she had *disappeared*. But *leaving*? That was
something she'd talked about all the time.

Getting out of Cheyenne and going to LA. Or
sometimes it was New York, or Paris if she were in
a romantic mood. For the first few days, that's what
Zachary had assumed happened. Because the night before, she'd come into his room after an argument with
their parents. (His mom hadn't told the police about
that, either.) She'd pressed her spine against his door
frame and closed her eyes. He always thought of her

as tall, since she was his big sister, but as an adult, he realized she'd been small. She'd closed her eyes and let out ragged breaths until she wasn't about to cry. Then she'd turned blazing eyes on Zachary and said, "Don't ever let them tell you who you are, Zachary. Don't let them poison you against yourself."

Zachary had never known exactly who his parents had tried to tell Sarah she was, and he'd forgotten the event over the years. But now, with the dreams recurring, he wondered again.

Bram had told him that Halloween traditionally marked a time when the veil between the living and the dead was thin. Zachary had never put much stock in such things, but in the week leading up to today, he'd wondered if perhaps there wasn't some element of truth—if not spiritual, then psychological—to Bram's explanation.

Because more than anything, it felt like Sarah was visiting him and telling him to take a chance on himself. To remain true to his own vision.

"Zachary. Baby. Are you okay?"

"Huh?"

He snapped back to the present to find Bram looking at him curiously.

"You seemed like you went away somewhere. What are you thinking about?"

"Do you believe in ghosts?"

"Mmm. I believe in energy, and the energy that life has. So it makes sense to me that energy could remain after someone's body was no longer living. And I definitely believe that people leave impressions on us long after they're gone. So the line between memory and ghosts is thin."

Zachary nodded.

"Are you okay?" Bram asked, cupping his cheek.

"Yeah." Zachary shook himself. "Yeah, I'm fine. Let's get started."

The install went better than Zachary had planned for. He supposed he'd planned for two of himself working on it, which meant he'd reckoned without Bram's seemingly tireless energy and strength. It was a little irritating how strong he was, honestly. Zachary grumbled at him as he just lifted basically a tree to reposition the dragon-cum-sea monster.

"I'm Bram, I'm Superman," Zachary muttered to himself.

Bram burst out laughing. Not exactly to himself, then, apparently.

"Aw, baby. Are you impressed?" He flexed his muscles in a way that was clearly self-mocking, but also legitimately impressive.

"No," Zachary lied.

Bram caught him up in his arms and kissed him sweetly, and Zachary felt some of his irritation drain away.

"Okay, okay," he said when Bram kissed all over his face. "It's fine that you're Superman."

"Well, you're Professor Xavier," Bram said.

"I'm not even a comics aficionado and even I know that *Superman* is DC and *X-Men* is Marvel," Zachary said.

"So what? I'm building bridges, baby." Bram grinned and kissed him again.

Chapter Twenty-Five

Bram

At four o'clock the children descended on Casper Road. In all the hullaballoo of setting up, Bram had forgotten that they would actually be expecting candy, so when Zachary had pulled the bags of sweets out of the cabinet, he'd zoomed to the nearest store and stocked up for his side of the street.

Zachary had shaken his head, but said, "This is why I built in a buffer." Then, screwing up his face, "Don't get any gross healthy candy, okay?"

He'd thought Zachary was exaggerating the amount he would need and resigned himself to eating candy for the next month. Now that he saw the hordes pouring in, he worried he hadn't gotten enough.

Hoot Owl Road, perpendicular to Casper Road, was

closed for parking and Casper Road itself was blocked off to all but pedestrian traffic, making a safe street for the kids to trick-or-treat on. The poles of all the streetlights had been draped with fake spiderwebs and their bulbs were wrapped in orange gels that cast globes of titian light on passersby. At the head of Casper Road, a plume of black and orange balloons bobbed in the breeze, marking the turnoff, and beneath it was a table piled high with jackets, the kids doffing them the second they arrived, happy to sacrifice warmth to display their costumes.

If the inhabitants of Casper Road went all out on the decorations, the trick-or-treaters matched their enthusiasm. With one glance, Bram took in an elaborate Batman, a Punky Brewster with a bandanna-ed dog in tow, and an extremely impressive Rubik's Cube that seemed to actually turn somehow.

Zachary had installed himself at the northwest corner of the yard, so that the audience (his word) could observe all the amazing things his house had to offer before they stopped to get candy. He didn't want them getting candy before they'd looked and then running off to the next stop without appreciating his hard work.

Bram was ardently anti-military, but he couldn't help but think that if apocalyptic war ever descended on Garnet Run, Wyoming, he would want Zachary at his side.

The last week had been a dream. He and Zachary worked so well together and had such fun that Bram never wanted the days to end—to say nothing of the steamy nights.

Zachary hadn't mentioned the promotion that week, but Bram could see him mentally chewing on it. He would get an intense distracted look, like he was focused on something internal, and fall silent for minutes at a time. His sleep had been interrupted too.

It had been killing Bram not to ask him every day what he was thinking about with regard to the future, but he'd held his tongue. He'd already given Zachary a hefty dose of his opinion and he knew some people needed a chance to process things on their own.

To distract himself, Bram had begun monitoring the cat shelters diligently over the last week, lining them with towels donated by shop owners on Main Street, putting out bowls of food, and checking to make sure there weren't wounded cats in need of medical care.

He'd added a hollowed-out tree trunk shelter to the clearing that held Wes Mobray's glowing trees, and when he'd checked that one he'd found two black cats in it, the glow of the plants reflected in their big eyes, tails twitching with interest as they gazed at the magical clearing around them. He'd taken a picture to send to Wes and also sent it to Rye. Rye had told him to send it to River, who managed the shelter's social media, and now it was up on their Instagram.

This had given Bram an idea. He didn't have any social media accounts, but he downloaded Instagram and began looking for architecture content. He found a whole community there of freelance designers who posted mock-ups of buildings they'd designed. On some of them, he'd seen comments by people who wanted to actually make the buildings a reality. As soon as they were done with Halloween, Bram was going to show Zachary and see if he wanted to post his own designs. They were so unique and creative, Bram felt sure there would be interest.

Suddenly, a terrifying monster jumped at him, claws out.

Bram lurched backward, clutching his heart. "Oh my god," he said, laughing when he realized the horrible monster was Gus Mills. "You scared me!"

"Yesss." She pumped her fist triumphantly.

"What are you?"

"I'm a cryptic mantis."

"Er. What is that?"

"It's a kind of mantis."

"Ah, of course. Well. You look extremely scary, if that's what you were going for."

"It was," she confirmed, clearly delighted.

Costume show-and-tell over, and Adam and Wes catching up to her, already wild-eyed, Gus began to look around her.

"Gus," Adam wheezed. "You skipped past all the other houses."

"Also when are the next track and field trials," Wes muttered.

"I wanted to see Bram," she said, shrugging.

She stood and gaped, clearly noticing the chainsaw-carved sea monster for the first time.

"Ohhh, that's so cool!"

She approached the sea monster and ran curious fingers over it.

"She insisted we get here as soon as it started," Adam said, clearly frazzled. "She's very enthusiastic about Halloween."

"So is Zachary," Bram said. "He even took the day off work. I didn't think he ever did that."

"He takes one day off a year for this when it falls on a weekday," Wes said.

"Where did you get this dragon?" Gus said, eyes wide.

"Oh, well, I made it. It's a sea monster, see?"

"How did you make it?"

"I carved it."

"Whoa. How?"

Wes blinked, remembering Adam's strict instructions to never tell her about chainsaw carving.

"With. Um. A feather?"

Wes snorted and Adam was clearly cultivating a studied neutrality.

Gus screwed up her face. "A feather? Feathers can't carve stuff."

"Right, um. With…" Bram was not a good liar. He wasn't good at making things up on the spot. So he went with a classic. "I can't tell you."

"What? Why?"

"Because."

"What's wrong with you?" Gus demanded.

"Gus," Adam said. "We do not ask people what is wrong with them."

Gus slumped. "Fine," she muttered. "But I *will* figure it out."

Adam's expression turned to one of terror and then settled into resignation.

"Look at the creepy decorations, Bug," Wes said. Finally, a distraction that worked.

The collaboration had turned out even better than Bram had expected, due mainly to Zachary's vision and planning.

In front of his own house, the green-and-black sea monster swam through an undulating blue tarp sea, and tentacles thrust up through it every five feet or so, dripping with green-black slime. Wes' bioluminescent algae tipped each tentacle with an eerie green glow.

The tarp continued across the street, visually signaling that his decorations and Zachary's were connected.

Gus followed the tarp and stopped in front of Zachary's house, gawking.

They had transformed the front into what looked like a cracked wooden hull studded with barnacles and overgrown with glowing green algae. From the cracks in the wood, bony appendages protruded, composed of an array of bones from different creatures that gave the effect of never-before-seen undersea-dwelling monsters burrowing through to Casper Road.

Bram actually didn't like to look at that part for too long because it was legitimately scary.

In the trees, other creatures lurked. The ghostly revenants of the ship's crew? Bloodthirsty pirates who met an unlucky end? It wasn't exactly clear and Zachary hadn't cared as much about the story as he had about the effect. Either way, they were situated so that they seemed on the verge of bursting from the trees to chase any hapless child who stumbled into their path in search of candy.

"Oh my god," Gus breathed. "That is so *cool*."

She ran up and started staring closely at everything, hands clasped behind her back as if she were already anticipating being told not to touch anything.

"Ask Zachary to tell you how he made the monsters," Bram called.

It would be Zachary's pleasure to explain in detail and would give Adam and Wes a chance to catch their breaths.

"Bless you," Adam said. "We've spent the whole week helping her with her costume and then she got home from school hyper on sugar because they gave them Halloween candy in class, and I swear she's got the energy of seven people."

Wes nodded. He was standing very still, hands in his pockets, scanning the crowd with just his eyes. Bram remembered Zachary telling him that Wes didn't enjoy crowds.

"Let me know if you'd like a break," Bram said quietly. "You can go hang out with Hemlock inside. My dog," he added.

"Thank you," Wes said avidly. "I'll let you know."

"This is truly incredible," Adam said. "I knew Zachary went all out on the decorations, but I honestly wasn't expecting something so elaborate."

"Yeah, he's pretty single-minded when he wants something," Bram said.

"Hey, Mathesons and company," Adam yelled, waving behind them.

Trooping down Casper Road were Jack Matheson and his partner, Simon, Charlie Matheson and Rye, Adam's sibling, River, and Henry and Cameron from the Odeon.

"Wow, queer Garnet Run, represent, huh?" Rye said, high-fiving Adam when they met.

"Seriously," said Jack.

Simon looked around with wide eyes, then tilted his chin to the ground.

"Where are your costumes, you assholes?" Rye asked. "I was explicitly instructed to wear a costume!"

"Er, what are you?" Cameron asked.

Rye glared. "I'm Theo Decker, the lead singer of Riven."

"Oh, right, yeah," he said with a smile. Then he peered closer. "Actually, you kinda look like him. I can't believe I never noticed."

"Riven?" Bram asked.

Henry shrugged.

"They're a band," Charlie said with the voice of someone who only knew because Rye had told him so.

"I swear some of you live under a rock," Rye said.

"I *thought* that was my brother I saw under that rock," Jack joked.

"How are the cats doing?" Simon asked River softly. The two of them stood next to each other, slightly back from the crowd.

"Good." River smiled as they thought of the cats. "There's this new little orange-and-white spotted cat that keeps coming up to the shelter on his own, and I'll let him in and give him some food and he'll let me pet him, but then he'll go stand by the door waiting to be let out again."

"He can't make up his mind?" Simon asked.

"Maybe. Or maybe he just wants both," River mused.

"What are you supposed to be?" Jack was asking Charlie.

"I'm a vampire. Obviously," Charlie said, indicating his cape and fangs.

Jack grinned and Bram smiled too. With his massive build, ruddy beard, and aura of extreme down-to-earth competence, Charlie was an extremely unlikely vampire.

Jack had dressed as Waldo from *Where's Waldo?*, and Simon was apparently a font. He was dressed in all black and had cardboard flourishes at his wrists and ankles and a black hat on. He stood with his legs together and held his arms out perpendicular to make the letter T. When he did so, Henry laughed, apparently delighted.

"I do enjoy a good serif," he said.

Henry's costume looked very familiar.

"Are you that Humphrey Bogart detective?" Bram guessed. His mom was very into classic noir films so he'd seen them often as a kid.

"Yes! Sam Spade."

Bram turned to Cameron, who was dressed in all black with a strange feathered hat.

"I'm the Maltese falcon," he said, rolling his eyes. "I told you no one was gonna get it," he told Henry, but he didn't seem upset.

River was dressed as a dreamy mermaid, in blue cloth that edged into silver. They had blue-and-silver glitter in their hair and their face was dappled with makeup so that it looked like scales. The effect was alien and beautiful.

Wes and Adam weren't in costume, and neither was Bram, so he supposed they were the assholes that Rye had been referring to.

Bram regretted not dressing up, but he'd been so busy lately he hadn't thought of a costume until today, at which point it was too late.

When he'd mentioned it to Zachary and asked if he had a costume planned, Zachary had sniffed, as if this were distasteful, and said, "I am not the attraction; the house is."

So that was that. But Bram decided that the next year he'd plan to dress up in harmony with whatever design scheme he and Zachary decided on for their houses.

Next year.

He hoped there would *be* a next year.

It was the most fun Bram had had since leaving Olympia. Somehow, he had managed to find a group of friends that he couldn't wait to get to know better. He loved the natural beauty of Wyoming and all it had to offer. He had the beginnings of a job doing something he truly cared about and would dive excitedly into running the catch and release program for Rye in November. He was learning that with a little space from his family, he was better able to pinpoint what *he* wanted, rather than depending on their responses to tell him.

And he had fallen in love with the sweetest, hottest, most brilliant, weirdest person.

The exact lines of the future might be up in the air, but finally, Bram knew what he wanted. And it turned out that having the blueprint for what you wanted and maybe being disappointed if you couldn't have it felt a hell of a lot better than the muddle of not knowing at all.

Five hours, ten pounds of candy, three temper tantrums, and one episode of vomiting later, it was time to bestow the award for best decorations.

Zachary had been in his glory all night, explaining their concept and decorations to anyone who asked with utter patience and as much enthusiasm the fiftieth time as he did the first.

Gus had begged to be allowed to stay until the announcement of the winner, and had happily stalked around the street with a notebook, refining her own metric for evaluation and hiding it from anyone who tried to peek. Wes had taken Bram up on his offer of sanctuary after an hour and when Bram had gone to check on him, he'd found him fixing his broken toaster with Hem looking on.

River had taken off after an hour to go tend to the kittens, but before they left they said, "What would you think about putting a camera up in one of the cat shelters and getting pictures and video for social media? It might encourage donations."

"That's such a good idea! I can rig a little stand for it that a won't be in the way if you let me know what kind of camera we'll be using."

River had smiled and ducked their head, eyes already full of ideas.

Henry and Cameron had left quickly, too, since there was an 8:00-p.m. double feature of classic horror films at the Odeon they needed to prepare for.

"Come if you dare," Henry had said with a rather chilling laugh. Bram shuddered. He was sure Zachary would be delighted.

Jack and Charlie Matheson had spent a long time walking up and down the street, heads close together, discussing something in low voices.

"Jack just signed a contract for a new graphic novel," Simon said quietly when Bram couldn't help but try and overhear what they were discussing.

"Oh wow, that's great."

"It's kind of about Charlie and Rye. Not like *that*," he said quickly when Rye raised an expressive eyebrow.

"It's really about Charlie more than me," Rye said.

"Maybe," Simon allowed. "It's about a man who loves to fix things and a man who has a house in need of fixing. And how they end up helping each other fix themselves."

Simon smiled a soft, proud smile.

"It's called *Best Laid Plans*. Jack just wants to make sure Charlie's okay with everything he plans to include."

"Just make sure Jack draws me super-hot, okay?" Rye said dryly.

"I'll make sure and pass that along," Simon said with a smirk.

Zachary had insisted that Bram stay in his yard for the duration of the trick-or-treating so that they could properly represent their houses and give out candy in a fair and balanced way (his words, obviously). Now, though, Bram crossed the street to where Zachary was standing, Adam by his side and Gus lying on her back in the tarp ocean, staring up at one of the creatures in the tree and trying to take pictures with Adam's cell phone.

"She started an Instagram," Adam said fondly.

"You should follow me!" Gus called. "I post the best pictures of tarantulas and snakes and..."

She rattled off a long list of things, but Adam whispered, "It's like ninety percent creepy bugs."

"Daddy doesn't like it cuz I sometimes forget to delete the pictures from his phone," Gus said apologetically.

"I go in there to look at a cute picture of my daughter and end up staring into the maw of a tarantula!"

"What's a maw?" Gus asked, screwing up her face.

"A scary mouth," Zachary said.

"Okay, well you should follow me on Instagram anyway," Gus said.

"I don't have an account," Bram said. "Sorry. It sounds great, though. I'll check it out."

"I like bugs. I'll follow you."

"Thank you, Zachary! I'm RealScientistGus."

Zachary took out his phone.

When the local news team assembled to make the announcement, the residents of Casper Road and all the trick-or-treating visitors still on-site gathered in the street.

"You nervous?" Bram asked Zachary.

Zachary snorted. "No."

"Ooh, overconfident, huh?" Bram teased, kissing him. "Maybe it's the Purcells' year!"

Zachary scoffed and kissed him again, then slid his hand into Bram's, bouncing in place with excitement.

Tamara Michaelson, the newscaster from KCWY, said a few words about the annual competition, then paused dramatically. Bram shoved his hands in his pockets and forced himself to act natural.

"And the winner of this year's competition…is house number 667, Bram Larkspur!"

There was a silence, and then scattered applause, but Bram only cared about one person's reaction.

Zachary's jaw dropped.

"Whaaaa?" he said to Tamara Michaelson, shocked. "Did you get confused—?!" Then he clamped a hand over his mouth for a moment. "I mean, um." He turned to Bram. "Congratulations?"

Zachary was so clearly forcing himself to say something nice but Bram could practically *see* him scanning both their houses trying to figure out how things could have gone so terribly awry.

Bram laughed, utterly delighted with Zachary's reaction and with himself for managing to keep the secret.

"Gotcha!" he said to Zachary, not able to wait one more moment for the reveal. "Final prank! I got them to say that. Oh my *god*, your face. I win the prank war!"

Zachary's eyes got even wider, and an impressed smile crossed his face.

"I can't believe you did that!"

"Yeah, Moon's gonna be so impressed. Also pissed because she just lost naming rights for her next dog to me."

It was a testament to how positive his sister had been that he wasn't going to be able to keep his final prank a secret that she'd accepted the bet.

"Wow," Zachary said. "I guess you found your competitive spirit after all."

"Learned from the best," Bram began, but he was interrupted.

"Just kidding, folks," Tamara Michaelson said. "The winner is…our first-ever joint victory, number 667 *and* number 666, Bram Larkspur and—for the seventh time—Zachary Glass, for the collaborative theme of Ghost Ship!"

Now the crowd cheered unequivocally, and Zachary leaned over, looking very pleased with himself. He brought his lips to Bram's ear and whispered, "I got them to say that."

Bram froze. Zachary had given up what surely would have been another solo victory to include him?

The crowd faded away. The street faded away. Everything that wasn't Zachary Glass receded into the distance.

Bram pulled him tight and looked into his eyes.

"I love you," he said. "I really...damn, I really love you."

He felt tears filling his eyes and Zachary's face went slack.

"You...you do?"

"Hell yeah, I do."

"But. But I. But I'm...me," Zachary concluded.

"Yup. Exactly. I love *you*."

"But."

Zachary didn't seem to have a follow-up to this, so Bram just gathered him in his arms and squeezed him tight. He didn't need Zachary to say it back yet. He didn't even need Zachary to understand. Because he, Bramble Larkspur, knew exactly how he felt and what he wanted, and he didn't need anyone else to tell him it was okay.

Chapter Twenty-Six

Zachary

The day after Halloween, winter swept through Garnet Run like it had been waiting in the wings.

Zachary didn't mind the winter, but this year it seemed incongruous. He'd never felt more like spring. Everything was changing, blooming, and he had a kind of energy that couldn't be contained.

Which came in handy, since taking down the Halloween decorations and cleaning up Casper Road after the insurgence of hundreds of candy-scarfing, litterbug children was significantly less fun than preparing for it.

One week after Halloween, on a cold Monday morning, Zachary was answering emails when Fisk requested a video chat.

Zachary's heart pounded.

The night before, he'd dreamed of Sarah again, but this dream hadn't left him shaken or afraid. In it, she'd been putting on makeup to go out with friends and he'd been sitting on her bed, watching the ritual of application as he often had.

She'd put on glossy red lipstick as a finishing touch, then kissed his cheek, leaving a lip print behind. "Love you, Z-man," she'd said before bouncing out the door.

He'd woken with the words echoing in his mind. The lipstick thing had actually happened several times, and he'd hated it. Hated the sticky feeling and the waxy residue left on his skin even once he'd wiped it off. But he'd never told her to stop because it was a ritual that was theirs alone.

That wasn't what stuck with him, though.

What stuck with him was the realization that Bram Larkspur had been the first person to say *I love you* to him since Sarah left.

"Morning, Glass," Fisk said. "Some points for the contract."

Bram had told him that doing things for outside approval wasn't a good way to be happy or do his best work. Bram had told him he wanted them to have a future together. Bram loved him.

"Morris, I need to interrupt you."

The man squinted into the camera. "What's that?"

Zachary looked at the rack of buildings that existed only on paper. At the beautiful work of his heart that Moray and Fisk had only ever asked him to make simpler, cheaper, more generic, *less* Zachary.

He imagined what it would be like to see one of *those* buildings in the world and it set his heart flying.

Anyone could design a box.

Only he could design these.

"Morris, I'm not taking the promotion."

He said it loudly and clearly, so there could be no mistake.

He expected to feel regret or panic. Uncertainty or fear.

But all he felt was relief and the glorious world of possibilities opening up around him.

Morris Fisk had clearly thought he was a fool to turn down the promotion, but his shrug of assent had been the nail in the coffin of Zachary's career at Moray and Fisk. Fisk didn't care that it be *him* becoming junior partner because Fisk didn't care about him, period. Or his work. He was a good candidate but there were others who would do just as well.

And for the first time, not being the best didn't make Zachary feel the compulsion to level up. Instead, it gave him utter clarity on his future. He didn't *want* to be the best in a place that didn't have the same standards or values or interests as he did.

What was the use of succeeding by a metric you didn't even value?

Don't let them tell you who you are.

Zachary knocked on Bram's door as soon as work was over for the day.

When Bram answered, looking rumpled and smelling deliciously of wood shavings, Zachary threw himself into his arms.

"Whoa," Bram said, catching him easily. "Hey, what's this?" He stroked Zachary's hair. "Come in, come in."

Something was different about the living room.

"You got a couch?" Zachary asked.

"Yup. It seemed like time."

"Can I sit on it?"

"That's kinda the point, love."

Bram sat on the couch and patted the cushion next to him. Zachary sank down, heart beating fast.

"I turned down the promotion," he said, and watched Bram's face light with hope. "I don't want to go to Colorado. I don't want to do *less* design; I want to do more. I don't want to turn my designs into watered-down, boring, generic crap that anyone could design. I want to see *my* visions become realities. I can't quit right away, obviously, because I need to make a budget and put a savings plan into place, but as soon as I have a timeline, I'll let you know so you can decide if it's acceptable to you."

Zachary congratulated himself on his full disclosure.

"Acceptable to me?"

"Yes, I realize that being gainfully employed and having access to the concomitant resources is something that our current relationship has been predicated upon and that disrupting that expectation might result in a change in your evaluation of its relative merits."

"What the hell are you talking about, baby?"

Zachary thought he had been quite clear and rigorous in his explanation. "As I said, you've made certain declarations predicated upon—"

Bram grabbed his arms and pulled Zachary into his lap. "Can you stop talking like an investment banker for a sec? I'm *so* proud of you for following your heart and not taking the promotion because it wasn't what you wanted. It seems really smart to make a budget and a plan before quitting your job. Now, what's all the rest of this about me?"

Zachary blinked. Was he really not being clear? "I…you said. You said you loved me."

Bram's eyes went soft. "Yeah, I did say that. And I meant it."

"You said that when I was maybe getting a promotion and had a steady job. I just want to make sure you know that I have plans to remain solvent once—"

"Hey, hey. Can I say what I think you're trying to say, and you tell me if I'm right?"

Zachary frowned, but Bram didn't seem upset, just exasperated. People often got exasperated with Zachary.

"Yeah, okay."

"I think maybe you're saying that you want us to be together and that if we're a couple then what affects you will affect me too, so you want me to know that you aren't suddenly going to have a very different financial situation than you do now because you don't want me to worry about you."

"Yes, isn't that what I just said?"

"Well, you said it without the part about wanting us to be together, so the context was a bit unclear."

"Oh."

Of *course* he wanted to be with Bram. Bram *loved* him.

But Bram was currently looking at him like he had still failed to supply critical information.

"Where'd you get the couch?"

"I found it at that weird antique store off Main Street. On a tip from Mrs. Lundy."

Zachary nodded. It was a nice couch. Not his style,

but it suited Bram with its soft neutrals and deep cushions.

"Um, so, if the plan is that you're going to try and quit your job once you have a, uh, a savings plan in place, can I show you something?" Bram asked.

"Sure."

Bram took out his phone and opened Instagram.

"I thought you didn't have an Instagram?"

"I don't. I just looked up some stuff. Oh, here. Okay. There's this whole hashtag for independent architects and they post what they're working on. I thought you might want to check it out. Some of the designs they post gain visibility and get commissioned to be built."

Zachary *pshaw*ed. It was cute when amateurs and students shared their work, but you didn't get structures built through Instagram.

"I know it's not your usual thing," Bram allowed. "But official channels aren't always the only way to effect change. You're used to having the firm as your liaison between design and execution, but that's not the only way it works. Not anymore. Here, look."

He scrolled through and tapped on a post. "This design was just constructed in Philadelphia. It's a low-income apartment complex with an exterior that looks like a larger version of the surrounding houses and has a communal courtyard and garden in the center that all the apartments look into."

Zachary peered at the design. It was cheeky and clever, the turn-of-the-century West Philadelphia duplex style scaled up to look like a world for giants. It was set back from the sidewalk so it wouldn't shade out the houses around it, and to encourage socializing in front of the building. The courtyard had zones of privacy due to the layout of hedges and benches, allowing it to function as a communal space while giving individuals a sense of ownership over the space.

It was truly lovely.

"This got built by posting it on Instagram?"

"Well, I think she posted it on Instagram because that's what her account is about, and found a community of people doing this kind of work and also looking for it."

"And you looked at this for me?"

"Yeah, of course for you. I want you to be able to keep designing your amazing buildings and I wanted to show you that working at a firm isn't the only way you can do that."

Zachary's mind was spinning. He'd never considered that he could do the work he loved outside the official capacity of a firm. Once, he would have dismissed the notion out of hand because he needed the structure and predictability that a firm provided.

Recently, though, he'd realized that he didn't have quite the same feelings he once did. More and more often, he'd been deviating from the structure he created for himself and it had been fine. More and more often, he'd thought about the future and felt curious about uncertainty rather than terrified. And when he traced it back to see when it had started…?

It had started with Bram. Lovely, sweet, kind, freewheeling Bram, who'd asked him to take twenty minutes off in the middle of the day to see the Purcells' surprise at their prank. Who'd pushed him gently and supportively to meet his family, even when he didn't know what was going on.

Who was always there, as strong and steady as a tree,

showing Zachary over and over that no matter what changed or went wrong, he would still be there. Now, Zachary thought, he could weather outside uncertainty because at the end of the day he'd come home to Bram.

Bram started to say something but stopped when he looked at Zachary.

Zachary looked directly into his eyes. "I love you," he said, as firmly and clearly as he could.

Bram blinked and then his eyes filled with tears. "Yeah?"

"Yeah, I—"

But Bram had grabbed him and clutched him like a teddy bear before he could explain his reasons.

He guessed maybe Bram already knew them anyway.

Zachary Glass had worshipped his sister. Her intelligence, her independence, her creativity, her take-no-shit attitude, her insistence on authenticity. In fact, Bram reminded him of her. He found himself thinking, as he nuzzled into Bram's strong shoulder, that wherever she was or wasn't, Sarah would approve of Bram. He thought she'd approve of his recent choice too—to take the path of creative freedom rather than one of banal safety. Maybe he even had enough of her take-no-shit attitude to thrive on that path.

But one thing he knew: he would not have to walk down it alone.

Chapter Twenty-Seven

Zachary

Six months later

The road stretched before them and behind them, a ribbon of black cutting through a world blushing green with spring.

Zachary had never taken a road trip before, to Bram's shock, so when they planned this trip to Olympia to visit Bram's family, they'd chosen to drive rather than fly.

As Bram pointed out, it was better for the environment anyway.

Bram seemed content to drive forever, which suited Zachary just fine, since he was enjoying staring out the window. The landscape itself was such an inspiration, with all its insights into form, structure, balance, and color.

As the sun set before them at the end of their first day on the road, it painted the land in red and orange, then slipped out of sight with a suddenness that surprised Zachary.

It was beautiful, but it also signaled the imminence of another thing Zachary had never done: camping.

They lugged their—well, Bram's—gear from the trunk to the campsite. Bram had a headlamp, which made things easier for him, but kept blinding Zachary when he swung around to look at him.

"You want to learn how to set up a tent?" Bram asked.

He seemed utterly at ease in this setting. In fact, one of the things Zachary appreciated more and more about Bram as he got to know him was that he seemed at ease everywhere.

Zachary sniffed. "I'm a trained architect, Bram. I'm sure I can figure out how to pitch a tent."

Bram grinned. "By all means, Mr. Architect."

Well, now Zachary had to do it. He examined the vinyl tube, the limp segments that he assumed supported it, and the stakes that must attach it to the ground.

Twenty minutes later, Zachary had put together his first tent and felt extremely pleased with himself.

"Ha!" he crowed at the tent.

Bram nodded seriously and stroked his chin. "Well, I'm very impressed with what you've invented here. Maybe it'll catch on. But, um. Not as a shelter."

Zachary examined what he'd created. It was rather low to the ground, sure, but wasn't that what camping was supposed to be all about—communing with nature or whatever?

"What's wrong with it?" he demanded.

"Well, aside from the extreme claustrophobia it would induce, nothing."

Fine, it was *very* low to the ground.

"These snap together," Bram was saying. In minutes, he'd turned the pleasingly geometric shelter that Zachary had constructed into something tall enough to stand in (if you were Zachary).

"Ah. Right. Okay."

"Now you know for next time," Bram said, and kissed him.

This was another thing he loved about Bram. He never made not knowing something feel bad.

They brought the rest of the supplies from the car and Bram started a fire. They'd stopped at a diner for dinner at Zachary's insistence because he said stopping at diners was in all the best road trip movies.

"Ready to make some s'mores?" Bram asked.

Zachary was very ready. Bram built a fire and they sat in the cool night air and watched it dance itself up into the sky.

Fire was something that had always fascinated Zachary. He wished he could figure out a way to make a structure that looked like fire.

Except, no. The most wonderful thing about fire was its wild unpredictability. To freeze that permanently in the form of a building and thus make it predictable, knowable, would violate everything he loved about it.

Now that Zachary was looking down the barrel of quitting his job, he found himself more inspired than ever. Inspired by everything, really, because the future was nothing but possibilities. He hadn't realized how habitual it had become for him to edit his ideas *as* he was having them, cutting them down to size from the beginning. Now he let them grow all the weird tentacles and beaks and claws they wanted.

He'd be giving his two-week notice when they got home from the Larkspurs'.

"S'mores are so good," Bram moaned, leaning into Zachary.

He had scorched his marshmallow black on the outside and left it gooey inside, and flecks of marshmallow char clung to his beard.

Zachary smiled and wiped them away.

"I was saving that for later," Bram said.

"You're such a dad," Zachary teased.

Bram grinned and winked. "You know it."

Zachary's own dad didn't make jokes. He didn't make much of anything.

Zachary had received several more calls from his mother over the last month, a sure sign she had another empty lead to dangle in front of him and another mission she wanted to send him on. He hadn't returned the calls.

"I'm worried they aren't going to like me," Zachary said.

"Aw, no way. They're gonna love you. I love you."

He said it as if it were truly that simple.

"I hope so," Zachary said, gnawing on a thumbnail.

"Have a s'more. They fix everything."

Zachary had a s'more.

He fell asleep to the sounds of crickets and the low

crackle of the flames, with the sweet marshmallow and chocolate taste of Bram's tongue in his mouth.

The Larkspur compound—because calling it a house would be an absurd miscategorization—was like nothing Zachary had ever seen.

Set back from town, down a winding road called Bramble Lane, the canopy of trees parted to reveal a rambling house, two outbuildings, a huge garden with raised beds, a chicken coop, and a pen for goats. The chickens and goats in question wandered around the meadow. One goat seemed perfectly at ease, standing at the fence line, looking into the distance with a chicken sitting on its head.

Bram had grown more and more fidgety with excitement the closer they got to Olympia, and now he let his joy flow out of him. Zachary had always gotten the sense that Bram's feelings were too big for him. But seeing him now, in this place, it was clear that they were the right size for Bram; Bram simply needed a bigger space to be Bram.

"Aww, Plastic Bag. She's such a sweetie."

"Your parents named their chicken Plastic Bag?" Zachary asked. "Why?"

"No, the goat."

"Oh, well, sure. That makes sense, then."

He'd been attempting sarcasm, but Bram seemed too blissed out by their arrival to take note of it. He said Zachary was bad at sarcasm anyway, since most things he said sounded sarcastic even when they were not. Zachary thought that was a problem of culture, not his intonation.

They only had a chance to make it halfway to the

front door when it opened, and Bram's parents came out.

"I'm so happy to see you," his mother said. His father wiped away a tear and pulled Bram into a bear hug.

Bram's father was taller than he'd seemed on video. About Bram's height, though not as broad. He had a full head of gray hair and blue eyes that snapped with intelligence from beneath wild eyebrows.

Bram's mother was also tall; she wore her gray-streaked blond hair in a messy bun and had soft brown eyes. She was wearing glasses and also had glasses pushed up on her head like a headband, as well as glasses hanging from a cord around her neck.

When Bram hugged her, he moved the hanging glasses so as not to squash them and tapped the ones on top of her head.

"Oh, there they are," his mom said.

She held Bram by the shoulders and looked at him intently.

"You look wonderful," she concluded. Bram grinned.

"Zachary," she said, turning to him just as warmly. "It's so wonderful to have you here. Hug?"

"Er, okay?"

She hugged him lightly—nothing like the fierce enfolding she'd given her son—and Bram's father did the same.

"Everyone will be here later," Bram's mother explained. "But there's plenty of time for you to get settled, have a rest, have a wander."

"Perfect," Bram said. "I want to show Zachary around."

The air was cool and sweet, and the sun shone gently

as they made their way around. Bram's mother told him about the garden and all that they were growing there. His father talked about the animals and the milk and eggs they got.

"Have you ever made cheese?" Zachary asked. It had always struck him as a fascinating process.

"I have! I make goat's milk ricotta and mozzarella regularly, but I have been wanting to try my hand at hard cheeses again."

Bram and his mother exchanged a look that Zachary couldn't read.

"Er, Dad once almost killed the whole family by feeding us a cheese he made. He'd aged it for six months, but the wax must've cracked because some mold got in and we didn't realize. We were all puking for a solid day."

He was grinning like this was a fond childhood memory.

"You're lucky you didn't start accusing each other of witchcraft," Zachary muttered.

Bram's father guffawed.

The land was beautiful, and Zachary felt immediately calm in the presence of Bram's parents. Like him, they were easygoing, generous, and gratifying conversationalists.

"So Bram tells us that you're interested in discussing solar energy," Bram's dad said.

"Yes. It's something that should be built into the original design of a building rather than added later, for maximum efficacy, and since I'm particularly interested in designs that interact with the landscape they'll end up in, it seems advantageous to have a strong working knowledge of the options solar power provides."

Bram's dad held out his hand, and Zachary took it after only a moment of hesitation, and let himself be educated in the ways of solar power.

Chapter Twenty-Eight

Bram

"My baby," his mom said as Zachary and his dad walked off. "I'm so glad to have you home. You know you're the last one I ever expected to leave town."

"I know. It's so good to be home."

He was desperate to know what his mom thought of Zachary. She certainly wasn't shy with her opinions. But she *had* just met him.

"Um," he said.

"I like him," she said with a wink.

"Oh thank god." He meant that she'd told him, but he was also grateful she liked him. "Tell me?"

"Mmm. He's intense. Genuine. *Not* funny," she added gently.

"No," Bram agreed and grinned. "Well, occasionally. But it's nearly always accidental."

"He seems," she said thoughtfully, "like someone who is always thinking, always innovating. Curious. I like that."

"Me too."

"He also seems very, very sad."

"Yeah. It's not sadness about anything now. Just a lot of sadness in the past," Bram said. "I think."

His mother put her palm to her heart. Bram had told her a lot about Zachary and knew she found his story heartbreaking.

"How is it going?" she asked, touching his arm and moving to walk through their raised beds, her favorite place to be.

"So good," he said. "My lease is up September 1st and I'm going to move in with him. I know what you're probably thinking, that it's fast and—"

"My Bramble. Don't ever assume that you know what someone else is thinking."

It was something his parents had often told them as children, and it was always a helpful reminder.

"Sorry, you're right. What do you think?"

"You don't care what I think, do you? You've made up your mind."

"Well. Yes."

"Good." She patted his shoulder. "It's very important for you to trust yourself."

"Yeah."

He was working on it. He hadn't quite realized the extent to which he looked for approval reflected back on him from his family's responses to his behavior. But once his dad had pointed it out, it was clear that having some space from them made it easier to check in with himself because there wasn't another Larkspur always looking over his shoulder, having opinions, and having known him since he was an infant.

"It's gonna be good. With us living together, we can split Zachary's rent, which will be cheaper, and will take some burden off Zachary since he's planning to quit the firm in a few weeks."

"That sounds very practical."

"Also, ya know, I'm wicked in love with him," he said with a wink and a grin, before bending to run his fingers over some seedlings poking their heads out of the dirt.

"Eggplant?" he guessed.

His mom's smile was wry. "You can always tell even before the true leaves come in. It's magic."

"Nah." He waved her off. They walked a little farther, then he said, "Wanna know my secret?"

"Yup."

"You rotate the crops counterclockwise—mostly— every year, on a five-year cycle. I just remember where you planted things in the past."

His mom shook her head. "That might be more impressive, actually."

"God, you want impressive, get Zachary to talk to you about architecture. He's so damn smart, and he has all these ideas about buildings that are gonna change the world."

Bram couldn't wait for Zachary to quit his job and devote all his immense creative energy to the kind of work that would satisfy him.

"I look forward to that," his mom said with a soft smile.

* * *

The Larkspur siblings weren't as many in number as the trick-or-treating mass that had descended upon Casper Road six months before, but they arrived with a similar impact, decibel, and hunger.

Zachary, Bram, and his parents were sitting out on the deck, and the calm was rent by their arrival.

"Little brother!" came the first call.

Bram stood and let Thistle ram into him and scoop him up in a bear hug, spinning them both around. Thistle was about the only person who had ever been able to do so, and Bram squeezed his brother tight.

"Missed you," he said when he could breathe again.

He got another squeeze.

Vega ran past him with a wave and called, "Gotta pee! I'll hug you in a minute!" and Bram grinned.

"Hey, Bumblebee," said Birch. She held his nieces' hands.

"Hey, guys!"

He hugged Birch, then squatted down to look at Millie and Dorothy. Even though he saw them often via the weekly family video chats, they were at an age where they looked different nearly every time he saw them.

They hugged him together, one on each arm, and he lifted them up and spun around until he felt dizzy. They seemed fine.

He staggered toward Moon, who had emerged from her truck bearing the familiar canvas bags that meant she'd brought bread.

She dropped the bread bags on the ground and launched herself at Bram. He barely caught her and they both went down in the grass in a pile of limbs and laughter.

"Okay, how's it going? Quick, tell me everything. You have six seconds," Moon said, exposing the ruse of their fall.

Bram burst out laughing. "It's going great, now get off me." He shoved his little sister just far enough away to get up, then pulled her back into a hug. "No, don't get off me. I've missed the hell out of you."

"Me too. I made your favorite."

His mouth watered at the thought of her honey wheat bread with herbs. "Thanks."

"Does he like bread?"

"Um. Yeah?"

She harrumphed and let him go.

Bram had just opened his mouth to yell a warning at Zachary when Moon launched herself at him. She skidded to a stop at the cartoonish look of horror on his face and opened her arms innocently.

"Hug?"

"Er. Okay." Zachary approached her as one would a particularly enthusiastic puppy that might cuddle you or might pee in your arms.

It wasn't an inappropriate response.

They settled in the living room that looked out over the garden. As always, his parents took the pink love seat by the fire, Thistle sat in the broken (by him) gray-and-blue houndstooth armchair by the kitchen, Birch and her kids sat on the beanbags by the window, and Moon and Vega threw themselves onto the large couch facing outside. Usually, Bram joined them, one on each side. But he wasn't sure if Zachary was up for snuggling with people he'd never met.

"Shove over a little," he told Moon and Vega. A pout flickered on Moon's lips but quickly disappeared. Bram sat next to them, and gestured Zachary to his other side. His boyfriend edged toward him warily, then sat down, sank deeper than he anticipated, and grabbed at Bram's shoulder.

Bram was very glad he'd asked for their first get-together to be siblings only. If significant others had come too, he could only imagine how overwhelmed Zachary would be.

"You doing okay?" he whispered, though with all the different conversations going on, he could've spoken at normal volume and not have been heard.

Zachary nodded slowly. "There are…quite a lot of you. And you're all very large."

Bram grinned.

He looked around at his family, in the place he'd always considered home, as the sun set outside over the garden he'd watched for his whole life, and had the strangest feeling.

This wasn't where he belonged anymore. At first it came on a wave of melancholy, but that was quickly replaced by a calm, quiet satisfaction. He didn't belong here anymore because he had finally found another place he belonged. He would always love his family, always return here, always remain close. But he had learned that he could thrive on his own, and it had given him a sense of cool distance that just made him appreciate even more that this place would always be here for him to visit when he wanted to.

He squeezed Zachary's hand and Zachary squeezed

back. Bram couldn't wait to see what kind of home Zachary would design for them.

The thought had dropped into his head as naturally as if it were guaranteed, but Bram knew it would happen. Zachary would consider every angle and measurement, every sconce and countertop. There would be vision and dream and future and…love. There would be love because Zachary loved him. His heart soared at the thought.

Something hit him in the face.

"Oy!" Thistle had thrown a hunk of bread at him.

"Sorry, did you say something?"

"That was made with my own two hands, ya lug," Moon scolded. Then *she* threw a hunk of bread at him.

Bram picked up the bread that had hit him and munched on it.

"Children, what will our guest think of us?" his mom said drolly. "Also, someone throw me a piece of bread. Or, you know, cut it up and get some butter and honey."

Thistle grumbled, but rose. If you started the bread fight you got the butter. Those were the rules.

A piece of bread sailed across the room and landed in his mom's lap.

"Nice throw," Bram told Birch. She winked.

"So, how is the grand transition going?" his dad asked Zachary.

"Excellent," Zachary said. "Well, I think so. It's not very quantifiable."

Since River was in charge of the social media for the Dirt Road Cat Shelter, they had taken it upon themselves to give Zachary a crash course. Simon, who did freelance graphic design, worked with Zachary on some branding.

"Tell them the name," Bram prompted.

"Glass Houses."

"That's great," Moon said. Everyone agreed.

"Actually, it's been very gratifying to look outside the official world of architecture—what's featured in the professional publications and lauded internally—and get a taste for what's being created by people who aren't working within the confines of budgets and client demands. It's like being back in school again. It's…" He looked self-conscious and Bram squeezed his knee. "I feel as though I've fallen in love with architecture again."

His face was lit with a smile that made Bram's stomach fizz.

Zachary had spent the last several months on an odyssey of realizing what he'd lost by stifling his creativity for the sake of his firm's requirements. The first few weeks he'd begun exploring others' work, he'd come to Bram every half hour or so, eyes wide and finger on his computer screen to show him something amazing that someone had designed.

"She designed it with *no walls*!" he'd say, then explain how the designer had done it. Or, "The entire house has trees planted inside it!" The innovations seemed to matter less in their particularities than the fact that people were doing things Zachary hadn't thought possible. At first, Bram had thought he felt competitive, as he so often had—annoyed or dispirited that these people had thought of things he hadn't. But it quickly became clear that he was *delighted*. Invigorated.

Inspired.

Zachary had become fast friends with Henry, discussing art deco (Henry's favorite style) and Henry's renovation of the Odeon and other theaters he'd worked on before settling in Garnet Run.

He'd also gotten close with Simon. Initially it was through Simon's help with his branding, but it turned out that they both enjoyed taking long walks, during which they hardly spoke, just appreciated the company.

For himself, Bram had been excited to get closer with Wes, bonding over a mutual passion for environmental solutions to problems, and enjoying tinkering with things.

Little by little over the last six months, in fact, he and Zachary had been spending time with (as Rye affectionately christened them) all The Queers of Garnet Run. Simon and Jack, Charlie and Rye, Henry and Cameron, River, Marie, who worked at Matheson's Hardware, and Jack's friends Rachel and Vanessa, not to mention a *lot* of animals.

It was starting to feel like they were creating a whole little family of their own. Every time they'd get home from spending time with them, Zachary would look a little spacey, as if he still weren't used to having friends that he saw regularly. But he was getting more confident in being himself with them the more he saw that they all liked him. In fact, Jack had said multiple times, "I can't believe I didn't know you before; this is so great."

Bram had also been spending more time with Mrs. Lundy, and when he met Simon's grandmother, Jean, and her friend Wayne, he did a friend fix-up of his own. Now, Jean, Wayne, and Mrs. Lundy could be seen around town making mischief at all hours. It made him happy to see it.

All in all, Garnet Run had begun to feel like home, not because of the place—although Bram loved the beauty of the landscape and the animals he could see there—but because of the friends he'd made.

And because of Zachary.

Zachary Glass who he fell a little more in love with each day. Zachary Glass who he couldn't wait to move in with. Who he couldn't wait to live with. Who he couldn't wait to wake up next to every morning for the rest of his life.

He looked at Zachary, appreciating the soulful dark eyes, the glorious curls, the somber set of his full lips, and the slight line that appeared between his expressive eyebrows when he was listening intently, as he was now.

Bram's mother was deep in the world of solar energy and Bram could see Zachary practically itching for a pad of paper to take notes.

God damn, he loved this man so much that seeing him with his family brought tears to Bram's eyes.

He blinked them away, relieved that Zachary was too focused on his conversation to see. Zachary still got nervous when Bram cried out of happiness because he hadn't realized it was a real thing until he met Bram.

But Moon reached over and wiped his cheek with her finger, expression tender.

"Oh, man, you've got it so bad, huh?" she whispered.

Bram bit his lip and nodded. "So, so bad." He grinned and Moon grinned back at him. She interlaced their fingers and squeezed, and he squeezed back and enjoyed watching his beloved boyfriend interact with his beloved family.

Chapter Twenty-Nine

Zachary

The Larkspurs were their own country. They were warm and welcoming, and Zachary knew that he was always only getting half of the currents that were lapping around him.

But it was fine, because Bram was home and Bram was happy, and Zachary had realized lately that he would do quite a lot to make sure Bram was happy. Including, apparently, drinking something that tasted like the bottom of a pond and answering some rather personal questions as, one by one, Bram's siblings each found a way to be alone with him when he was on his way to the bathroom, or got water (to wash down the pond-drink), or looked at the garden.

When Moon, the final sibling to have her go, intercepted him in the hallway, he said, "You all should've coordinated your efforts."

"Huh?" she said, feigning innocence.

"You should've just decided on all the questions you wanted to ask me beforehand, and sent a delegate."

Moon looked mildly abashed.

"You, uh, got asked these things before?"

"Yes. By all of you. The whole brood."

"Oh." She narrowed her eyes, evaluating him. "You mad?"

"Nope. I know you love Bram. Just sick of answering the same questions. I should've just addressed the whole family: *Yes, I love Bram and swear to be good to him. Yes, we're moving in together. Yeah, I don't like dogs, but I promise I'll be nice to Hemlock anyway. Yes, he's great in bed, I'm sure you're all very proud.*"

Moon's eyes got wide. Zachary had not intended to say that last part out loud.

"Er. I did not intend to say that last part out loud."

Moon laughed and clapped him on the back.

"Sorry," she said. "It's just that Bram really—"

"Got hurt terribly when his boyfriend and best friend betrayed him. Bram is a sweet, kind, trusting soul who needs to be protected. Did I get that right?"

Moon blinked. "Well. Yes."

"Great. But here's the thing. Bram doesn't need to be protected. He's strong and resilient and everyone gets hurt, but he got through it and he's fine. I'm his boyfriend, not his parent. I don't need to protect him from the world because he can protect himself. He's not a child who doesn't know how things work. He's trusting because he enjoys the feeling of trusting people. Must be nice. Anyway. I know you all mean well, but the best thing you could do for Bram? Is stop trying to run interference between him and the world."

Moon's eyes had gotten even wider as he spoke, and when he finished, he realized his voice had risen in volume and the living room had gone silent for the first time since they'd all arrived.

"Um," Moon said.

Arms came around Zachary's chest and he was hugged from behind. He let himself melt into Bram's strong chest and breathed in his smell.

"Thank you," Bram said seriously.

Zachary turned and saw Bram's eyes glowing with love and unshed tears.

The mythical "happy tears," which he'd read about but never believed were real until meeting Bram.

"You weren't supposed to hear that," Zachary muttered.

But Bram just squeezed him tight and kissed his temple.

When they went back into the living room, every Larkspur's gaze was on him. He tensed, but as he looked closer at their expressions, he saw they weren't hostile or defensive. They were happy, gratified, a little ashamed, surprised, and impressed, respectively.

"Is this your childhood bedroom?" Zachary asked.

The eating, drinking, and talking had gone on for hours and Zachary had gotten exhausted with it after a while, and simply put his head in Bram's lap and gazed out the window at the garden lit with solar-powered fairy lights. It was beautiful.

Now the crowd had dispersed, and Bram had shown him to a room draped with tapestries and plastered with band posters and stickers, and cluttered with vases of dried flowers, books, art supplies, and wood shavings.

"Yeah, kind of. There are four rooms besides my parents', so we kind of swapped around who shared with who, and who got their own room over the years and when we started moving out one by one. This was my room most recently, but I think Moon stays in here a lot when she comes to hang out and doesn't want to drive home. She and my dad have gotten into whiskey tasting."

Zachary shuddered at the thought of the already brash Moon intoxicated.

They brushed their teeth in a small bathroom in the hallway that was packed with plants. The toothpaste tasted weird.

In the bedroom, Bram had opened the window and cricket song poured in with the breeze. It smelled of ozone and moss and dirt and made Zachary feel instantly sleepy.

The bed was small, and Bram was large, so they ended up wrapped tight together with the worn, homemade quilts that smelled of cedar tucked up to their chins against the fresh, cool air.

Bram stroked his hair. With his ear to Bram's chest, he could hear the slow and steady thump of his heart. It beat so steadily that Zachary sometimes thought, as he drifted off, that it was the only truly dependable thing in the universe. And he was so very glad that it was his.

"How are you doing, baby?" Bram asked. "I know today was a lot."

"I'm so comfortable," Zachary murmured, snuggling closer.

"Good."

They lay like that for a while, Zachary's mind ranging back over the conversations he'd had with Trent and Mirabelle about solar paneling and a design he was currently working on, the way Bram's rough fingers had run so tenderly over the seedlings in the garden, and the smell of the country air lulling him to sleep.

"Would you want to live in the country?" Zachary asked carefully.

"Yeah," Bram said without hesitation. "I like to be within close driving distance to things, but I would love to have a plot of land. Enough to grow vegetables, have a few animals. Wander around naked whenever I feel like it." He squeezed Zachary's butt.

"You basically do that now," Zachary muttered.

"Shirtless is not naked, darlin'," Bram said breezily.

Zachary thought hard.

"Enough space that some of your family could stay when they came to visit. A woodshop like Charlie's."

Bram turned on his side and gathered Zachary even closer.

"That sounds like heaven."

Zachary's heart pounded. "I could design that. I could design whatever you wanted."

Bram kissed him. "Whatever *we* want."

"Yeah?" Bram sounded so certain.

"*Hell* yeah. Of course, baby. I'd love that. Don't you know that?"

Zachary dragged himself up and leaned against the wall. Bram sat up too. The moon was nearly full and once his eyes adjusted, Zachary could see Bram's face in the silvery light.

Bram ran a finger over Zachary's eyebrow and nose and lips.

"I would love to live in a house that you designed for us, on some land, near Garnet Run. Or anywhere. It would make me so happy to build a life with you."

Bram was looking at him intently and Zachary's heart was hammering in his chest.

"For—for a long time?" Zachary choked out, squeezing his eyes shut at the word that had almost escaped.

The blankets shifted and Zachary smelled Bram close, so close. Bram kissed one eyelid and then the other, and Zachary opened his eyes. Bram's were burning with love. His own, he realized with shock, were burning with tears.

"Forever, Zachary Glass. I want to build a forever life with you."

The word didn't stick in Bram's throat, but floated out, as weightless as blown dandelion puff; as certain as its seeding.

"Forever." He tried the word out, its angles unfamiliar on his tongue. He had never thought about forever. Nothing had ever been forever before.

The word erased every bit of his exhaustion and replaced it with a giddy, electric sense of possibility.

"What else would you want in the house?" Zachary asked, practically bouncing on the bed.

Bram's smile was so big and so sunny it took Zachary's breath away. Bram brushed the forgotten tears from Zachary's eyes and Zachary kissed him and squeezed him so tight he lost his breath for a moment.

"I would love a porch. Like a big, wraparound porch where we could sit and have coffee in the morning or tea at night."

Zachary nodded. He would use a wood that would blend in with the surrounding land so it would look almost like nothing was there at all.

"What else?"

"A fireplace in the living room. A big one, so we could curl up in front of it and watch it all winter long."

Zachary could see the natural stone hearth that would be made of rock native to Wyoming. Bram would like that. Then he remembered it was supposed to be *their* house, and added a hand-milled mantel with midcentury lines. Maybe he could hire Charlie to build it for them.

"I need to write all this down," Zachary said.

Bram rolled off the bed and rummaged through the drawers of the oversized desk shoved under the window. He pulled out balls of string and piles of photographs, and odds and ends that Zachary had no hope of naming. Finally, he came up with a black-and-white composition notebook and a gnawed-on pencil.

"Okay," Zachary said, and flipped open the book to start sketching.

But the notebook wasn't empty. The first few pages were in a large, scrawling hand that Zachary recognized as a less refined version of Bram's penmanship.

"Oh my god, this is from high school," Bram said. He tapped the page. "Marcus Ling, he was in my sophomore history class and I had such a crush on him."

Bram slung an arm over Zachary's shoulder to better read his old journal.

Pumpkins are coming up finally. I hope the casperi-

tas don't rot this time. I mulched them so that should help. Marcus is my partner for the history project. I hope we can work on it alone. But we should go to his house because Birch and Moon are so embarrassing lately. Winnie let me pet her this morning on the way to school.

"Who's Winnie?"

"Winnie was this horse that our neighbor used to have. The fence ends at the road and she would stand there and look over it as we walked to school. Usually if we got too close she'd shy and run away. But if we were really quiet, or I was by myself—because we were never quiet—then sometimes she'd let me creep up to the fence and pet her nose."

Zachary pictured Bram, tall for his age, running late for school where he'd get to see his crush, checking on pumpkins and petting horses' noses, and it filled him with such tenderness he felt the pricking of something that might just be a cousin to happy tears.

Somehow, knowing that Bram was still Bram when he a teenager made him feel safe.

The rest of the page outlined some inter-sibling feud that even Bram couldn't parse, then before the rest of the notebook's blank pages, there was a sketch of a bear cub.

"Did you do that?"

Bram squinted at it. "I think so, but I don't remember. I did have this thing as a teenager where I really thought if I could just hug a bear it would be my friend and, like, walk to school with me and stuff."

Zachary laughed. "That is not an accurate impression of bears," he said, but he said it gently.

"Yeah. Well. I'm a romantic." Bram winked at Zachary and then turned to a fresh page of the journal.

Zachary had never kept a journal. He'd never had any interest in recording the happenings of his life. After all, who would want to go back and read a tale of bullying, teasing, tormenting, disappearance, death, and loneliness?

Certainly not him.

But seeing the words of this long-ago Bram made him certain somehow that they would have been friends.

"I wish I'd known you in high school," Bram said, as if he'd plucked the thought from Zachary's very brain. "I would've kicked the asses of everyone who was mean to you." His voice went fierce.

Zachary smiled. "I never took you for much of an ass-kicker."

"Well, no, okay. But I would've been tall at them and told them they were making really terrible choices."

Zachary laughed. "Thanks, I'm sure that would've left quite an impression."

Bram nodded sincerely and Zachary kissed him.

"Thanks. For real."

"You're welcome," Bram whispered. "Now draw me our house."

Zachary didn't think. He didn't edit. He didn't consider innovation or the opinions of anyone who would see it. He just let lines flow onto the page that reminded him of Bram. Of him. Of him and Bram together. Obtuse angles, gentle curves, solid, earthy materials, light glass. Earth tones at the bottom, sky tones at the top.

They talked about marble and tile and wood, ceiling heights and bay windows and skylights. Zachary drew room after room, garden after garden, each one circling closer and closer to a dream. To a promise. To a life.

"I want to wake up with you in our bed and look out the window as the sun rises," Bram said.

Zachary made a note that the bedroom should be east-facing and Bram kissed his neck.

"I want to leave you still sleeping in bed and go work on carving, knowing you're all warm and cuddly under the covers."

Zachary made a note that the woodshop should be as far away from the bedroom as physically possible. Bram kissed his temple.

"I wanna go pick vegetables and herbs from the garden and make you dinner that we can eat on our porch and watch the sun set," Bram said.

Zachary noted that the kitchen should have a door leading to the garden and that the dining room should flow into the porch facing west.

Bram kissed him deeply.

Bram understood that this was the language he used to say *I love you*. That he would design a house so perfectly in tune with the life they wanted that it could usher it into being.

They used page after page of the notebook, kissing between brainstorms. Zachary had never felt more exhilarated about a project. He supposed because he'd never thought of living inside one before.

They talked through the night, and as the first blush of morning fell through the window, Bram took his hand.

"Come with me?"

They got dressed and Bram grabbed two of the blankets off the bed. Zachary grabbed the notebook.

They crept through the house and out the back door. The garden was bathed in the softest light—half moon, half almost sun. Bram squeezed his hand and they settled on a bench next to the tomato plants. Zachary shivered and Bram wrapped the quilts around him, then wrapped his arms around the quilts.

"Sit with me."

They sat on the bench. The sky lightened with every passing moment.

"Thank you for coming here with me," Bram said. "It means so much. But I can't wait to get back to *our* home. Our life."

Zachary's heart fluttered at the thought.

"Monday's the day." He was giving his two-weeks' notice.

Bram nodded and squeezed him. "I'm so proud of you."

An orange-and-black butterfly fluttered down and landed on a plant.

"That's milkweed," Bram said. "Can we have that in our garden? It's the only thing monarch butterflies eat."

Zachary added it to the list of plants and flowers they'd begun inside.

"Oh, and dahlias. I love dahlias. Do you like dahlias?"

Zachary didn't know what dahlias looked like, but he leaned against Bram's strong shoulder and gazed out at the garden.

"We should have a huge window in the kitchen so

we can look out at the raised beds," Zachary said, extracting one arm from the quilts to sketch it in.

"That sounds perfect," Bram said.

They sat on the bench in the garden at the Larkspur compound, pressed close together against the morning chill. And as a new day dawned around them, they planned the life that they would have together in the old notebook. Past, present, and future cohering into the gentle whisper of the land: *yes*.

* * * * *

WE HOPE YOU ENJOYED
THIS BOOK FROM

HARLEQUIN
SPECIAL
EDITION

Believe in love. Overcome obstacles. Find happiness.

Relate to finding comfort and strength in the
support of loved ones and enjoy the journey
no matter what life throws your way.

6 NEW BOOKS AVAILABLE EVERY MONTH!

#2941 THE CHRISTMAS COTTAGE
Wild Rose Sisters • by Christine Rimmer
Alexandra Herrera has her whole life mapped out. But when her birth father leaves her an unexpected inheritance, she impulsively walks away from it all. And now that she's snowed in with West Wright, she learns that lightning really *can* strike twice. So much, in fact, that the sparks between them could melt any ice storm...if only they'd let them!

#2942 THANKFUL FOR THE MAVERICK
Montana Mavericks: Brothers & Broncos • by Rochelle Alers
As a rodeo champion, Brynn Hawkins is always on the road, but something about older, gruff-but-sexy rancher Garrett Abernathy makes her think about putting down roots. As Thanksgiving approaches, Brynn fears she's running out of time, but she's determined to find her way into this calloused cowboy's heart!

#2943 SANTA'S TWIN SURPRISE
Dawson Family Ranch • by Melissa Senate
Cowboy Asher Dawson and rookie cop Katie Crosby had the worst one-night stand ever. Now she's back in town with his two babies. He won't risk losing Katie again— even as he tries to deny their explosive chemistry. But his marriage of convenience isn't going as planned. Maybe it's time to see what happens when he moves his captivating soul mate beyond friendship...

#2944 COUNTDOWN TO CHRISTMAS
Match Made in Haven • by Brenda Harlen
Rancher Adam Morgan's hands are full caring for his ranch and three adorable sons. When his custody is challenged, remarriage becomes this divorced dad's best solution—and Olivia Gilmore doesn't mind a proposal from the man she's loved forever. But Adam is clear: this is a match made by convenience. But as jingle bells give way to wedding bells, will he trust in love again?

#2945 SECRET UNDER THE STARS
Lucky Stars • by Elizabeth Bevarly
When his only love, Marcy Hanlon, returns, Max Tavers believes his wish is coming true. But Marcy has different intentions—she secretly plans to expose Max as the cause of her wealthy family's downfall! She'll happily play along and return his affections. But if he's the reason her life went so wrong, why does being with him feel so right?

#2946 A SNOWBOUND CHRISTMAS COWBOY
Texas Cowboys & K-9s • by Sasha Summers
Rodeo star Sterling Ford broke Cassie Lafferty's heart when he chose a lifestyle of whiskey and women over her. Now the reformed party boy is back, determined to reconnect with the woman who got away. When he rescues Cassie and her dogs from a snowstorm, she learns she isn't immune to Sterling's smoldering presence. But it'll take a canine Christmas miracle to make their holiday romance permanent!

SPECIAL EXCERPT FROM

(H) HARLEQUIN

SPECIAL EDITION

By the book success story Alexandra Herrera's got it all mapped out. But when her birth father leaves her an unexpected inheritance, she impulsively walks away from her entire life! And now that she's snowed in with West Wright, she learns that lightning really can strike twice. So much, in fact, that the sparks between them could melt any ice storm…if only they'd let them!

Read on for a sneak peek at
The Christmas Cottage,
the latest in the Wild Rose Sisters series
by New York Times *bestselling author Christine Rimmer!*

So that was an option, just to say that she needed her alone time and West would intrude on that. Everyone would understand. But then he would stay at the Heartwood Inn and that really wasn't right…

And what about just telling everyone that it would be awkward because she and West had shared a one-night stand? There was nothing unacceptable about what she and West had done. No one here would judge her. Alex and West were both adults, both single. It was nobody's business that they'd had sex on a cold winter night when he'd needed a friend and she was the only one around to hold out a hand. It was one of those things that just happen sometimes.

It would be weird, though, to share that information with the family. Weird and awkward. And Alex still hoped she would never have to go there.

"Alex?" Weston spoke again, his voice so smooth and deep and way too sexy.

"Hmm?"

"You ever plan on answering my question?"

"Absolutely." It came out sounding aggressive, almost angry. She made herself speak more cordially. "Yes. Honestly. There's plenty of room here. You're staying in the cottage. It's settled."

"You're so bossy…" He said that kind of slowly— slowly and also naughtily—and she sincerely hoped her cheeks weren't cherry red.

"Weston." She said his name sternly as a rebuke.

"Alexandra," he mocked.

"That's a yes, right?" Now she made her voice pleasant, even a little too sweet. "You'll take the second bedroom."

"Yes, I will. And it's good to talk to you, Alex. At last." Did he really have to be so…ironic? It wasn't like she hadn't thought more than once of reaching out to him, checking in with him to see how he was holding up. But back in January, when they'd said goodbye, he'd seemed totally on board with cutting it clean. "Alex? You still there?"

"Uh, yes. Great."

"See you day after tomorrow. I'll be flying down with Easton."

"Perfect. See you then." She heard the click as he disconnected the call.

Don't miss
The Christmas Cottage *by Christine Rimmer,*
available November 2022 wherever
Harlequin Special Edition books and ebooks are sold.

Harlequin.com

HSEEXP0922